PRA

MW01267967

"*My Shadow Book* contains multitudes. It's a fascinating collage of quotations, diaries, drawings, aphorisms, confessions, short fictions, and political manifestos. Concealed within is a clever Mobius strip narrative and an invitation to a secret society comprised of history's most subversive artists. It's many potential books in one, waiting only for a reader to bring it to life."
—Jeff Jackson, author of *Mira Corpora* and *Destroy All Monsters*

"Jordan Rothacker's ebullient, entrancing, playful, linguistically sensuous *My Shadow Book* is a triumph of narrative and structural inventiveness. As the intrigues and mysteries unfold, Rothacker's polyphonic storytelling becomes a journey of ever-increasing entrancement. Invoking the epic speculative works of Clarice Lispector, Milorad Pavic, Edmond Jabés, and Borges, *My Shadow Book* is a masterfully crafted kaleidoscopic reinvention of literary beauty: a fragmented, arcane, haunting, and deliciously luxurious complexity of shimmering light that illuminates the very edges of thought and language."
—Quintan Ana Wikswo, author *A Long Curving Scar Where The Heart Should Be*

"In the sublime *My Shadow Book*, Rothacker carefully traces an aesthetic genealogy of shadow-thinkers, deftly fusing it to his own narrative. The end result is stunning, mesmerizing, an idiosyncratic mythology, reminding us of the possibilities of what this strange thing we call 'a book' can be. Rothacker offers up a graceful and radical counter-poetics to give the reader deep

and serious pleasure in our troubled times."
—Alistair McCartney, author of *The Disintegrations*

"Part farce, part gumshoe noir, part deep inquiry into the nature of belief—*And Wind Will Wash Away* is all of these things and more. Under Jordan Rothacker's pen, the American South is rendered an absurd and mystical topography that brings to mind such writers as Thomas Pynchon, James Purdy, David Foster Wallace, William S. Burroughs, and David Lynch. Be prepared for a crazy, inspired, breathtaking ride."
—Christian Kiefer, author of *One Day Soon Time Will Have No Place Left to Hide.*

"Any book blurb serves two functions: (1) Contextualizing of a work. (2) The lending of authorial imprimatur. *And Wind Will Wash Away* is too huge, too sprawling, too complex, too interesting and too weird for pithy contextualization. So here's what I'll say: I really, really, like this book."
—Jarett Kobek, author of *I Hate the Internet*

"You'd be hard-pressed to find a more literary, erudite and metaphysical noir novel than the one now in your hands. Detective Jonathan Wind's search for the killer of his beloved mistress, Flora Ross, leads him through history, literature, art, and an Atlanta that swirls with ghosts, tricksters, demons, saints and a phantasmagorical array of urban characters you haven't seen since Fellini filmed his dreams and nightmares of Rome."
—Reginald McKnight, author of *White Boys and He Sleeps*

GRISTLE

Stalking Horse Press
Santa Fe, New Mexico

GRISTLE
WEIRD TALES

JORDAN A. ROTHACKER

STALKING HORSE PRESS
SANTA FE, NEW MEXICO

Temp passé Trépassés Les dieux qui me formâtes
Je ne vis que passant ainsi que vous passâtes
Et détournant mes youx de ce vide avenir
En moi-même je vois tout le passé grandir

—"Procession" by Guillaume Apollinaire

CONTENTS

DEDICATED TO

JESSICA ERIN

AND

WEST PRICE,

WHO TOOK DICTATION ACROSS KANSAS WHILE I DROVE AND WROTE
"OOH OOH, THAT SMELL" AND WHO MODELED FOR STEW FISH IN
"SOMETHING THAT HAPPENED A LONG TIME AGO."
HE WAS MY FRIEND AND I'LL MISS HIM FOREVER.

TAKING THE BONE

FROM 'IN THE CANCER OF IT ALL'

THE ABORTIONIST voted for George W. Bush. That day she had received the new Jane Magazine and the horoscope told her to "Try something different today, surprise yourself." She wasn't surprised when he won and looking back she naturally assumed it was her vote that put him in, even though he lost the popular vote; she knew the use of her powers always created greater conflict in her life. As it was the first time she ever voted, it was exactly the way her luck worked.

The plastic keys were tough beneath her fingers. She pounded hard at her sexual memoir, pounding harder at her sexual memory. The working title was "Taking the Bone" and it was not intended to be pornographic or clinical. Really, it veered from the erotic by quite a bit and she liked to refer to it as "rhapsodic," though if the reader did not pick up on that she would settle for it to be perceived as a "lament."

The title came the way of all double entendres, in a flash of visceral smut. Looking back over the years and the penises, or bones, she accepted and took them for all they were worth, she saw them all as one violent stream of insertions, and over other words like cock and hammer, bone stood out the most in viewing this thought reel, and sent her into another image. The image at the end of the semiotic chain was from Stanley Kubrick's *2001*, where at the beginning of the film the ape/man hominid lifts his arm to the mighty beats of Strauss and takes hold of power by taking hold of the bone. So in writing her sexual memoir under this title, she is aligning herself with her most primal image of empowerment.

Out the window she looked as she typed, the parking lot all but empty, the sun piercing. A distraction was what she sought in her memoir, her sexual past, a distraction from what is supposed to be her true work. By day the Abortionist was a full-time student at work on a Master's degree in History, specifically the history of the nation-state. Another study of power to occupy her time. One could say she was a student of power. She was most intrigued by the fleeting quality of power, its fickleness and fragility. In Riasanovsky's *History of Russia*, a class text, she hones in on a line on page 16 about the Avars: "Their invasion is dated AD 558, and their state lasted for a century in Russia and for over two and a half centuries altogether, at the end of which time it dissolved rapidly and virtually without a trace, a common fate of fluid, politically rudimentary, and culturally weak nomadic empires." The notion, not of genocide, but of the extinction of an empire was a marvel to her. The people who were once Avars might have seed in someone, but their power and might as a people were gone. They were conquerors conquered by no one but themselves, and in a history of their once conquered lands they occupy less than a paragraph.

Summer heat on the other side of the window is an alien concept when the conditioned air blows. The Abortionist sat under the vent; it was the best view for her desk. The cold blow of the air chilled her in its mechanical intervals. Her nipples hardened bra-less against her thin tank top and she pulled over her head the light sweater from the floor next to her. When the blowing ends she will take the sweater off; the cycle is further distraction. The moments before the sweater gets over her head she is fueled in the work of her memoir with the prickling feel of her nipples against her top. The shiver of goose flesh that the cool air runs over her arms, neck, and loose breast intensifies the feeling of "being in" her own skin. The auto-erotica continues momentarily within the sweater as the new heat around her breasts relaxes the contracted flesh from the nipples, allowing the expanding and loosening area to touch more of her top's texture.

The Abortionist wishes there was a way to bring both of these pursuits together into one discipline. So far she has found no place in the history of the nation state for her sexual memoir and no place in her sexual memoir for the history of the nation state, unless of course she slept with her Thesis Advisor. Maybe she should have pursued a degree in Woman's Studies or something more Postmodern, like Critical Theory. This thought of unity is just another distraction, but it has merit. Each bone she ever took is a history unto itself; some repeated penetrations onto the same shaft would necessitate a 726 page volume like Riasanovsky's work, while some random insertions would require no more space than what he spent on the Avars. Yet each one was a conquest, each she notes, was an empowerment; they didn't give it to her, she took it from them. She was never a tyrant, but conquest has its price. Where are all those bone-bearers now while she sits here alone composing her history? It is known that history is written by the victors.

She writes on, her skin tightening, air-conditioning blowing down on her, its sound carrying down from on-high the silent screams of her death-born children, to her the fevered pitches of triumphant glee.

PARABLES THREE

1.

ONCE, MANY YEARS FROM NOW, a boy will gaze out into the desert night at a huge hollow bowl-shaped plateau. The boy's curiosity will be stirred. After journeying to the top of the structure, the boy will encounter an old man. When the boy asks the old man why the structure is shaped in such a way, the old man will motion for the boy to sit and at once begin to tell his story.

"Many years ago there was a President in office, not very different from the president that we have now. The president had a wife with quite a reputation for tragically bad luck. Once, at a moment of utmost despair and frustration, the wife shook the walls of the White House with a bellow of 'God Damn It.' God did not take such a blasphemous outburst kindly and smote the first lady, leaving a pile of ash and jewelry on the carpet of the Oval Office. When the President returned, he found the charred remains of his wife and knew immediately who was responsible. The President vowed revenge. For months the President tried to get a declaration of war against God passed in Congress, but kept reaching a stalemate between the Senate and the House. The President realized that he needed to take matters into his own hands. So he called the CIA, who put together a crack team of mercenaries and launched an assault on Heaven. A ferocious battle began and lasted many years ending finally with the CIA victorious. God was decapitated and fell from heaven. His body sank into a trench deep in the ocean and his head landed in the desert here beneath me."

When the boy hears the last of the old man's story, he will climb down from the dilapidated mass and go off into the world. After many years, the boy will return, all grown up and leading a construction crew. The old man will be there no longer, and the boy will put up a gate around the plateau. On, around, and amongst the plateau, the boy builds an amusement park. People come from miles around to buy a ticket and wait in line for admittance to the park. In front of the park the boy posts a sign that says: "Come Ride the 'God's Skull' Cyclone!"

2.

THE MAGICIAN scuttled into town and began selling his potions. By nightfall, all the vials of transformation potions were sold. The magician, being old, began to doubt himself. He remembered the hope in the purchasing faces and his esteem shriveled up into his stomach. He scurried about the residential area dripping with anxiety and muttering to himself. Entering a neighborhood, he found a customer's house.

"It's not going to work it's not going to work it's not going to work," babbled the magician as levitated up to the window.

Inside, he saw an enormously obese man with one of the vials of transformation potion. The man swallowed the potion and nothing happened. The obese man began to curse the magician and weep.

"I'm a failure. I knew it wouldn't work. I'm nothing," whined the magician as he reluctantly aimed his finger, sending a beam of light from its tip to the obese man, making him thin and attractive.

The newly thin and attractive man, oblivious to his current state, continued to voice his hatred and his regret about encountering the, as he stated, "worthless" magician.

"Bah!" screamed the magician, grieved by his failure, as he dropped down to the ground.

The magician proceeded to the next house that appeared to belong to a customer. He crept through the backyard, invisible to the guard dog, and peered in the back window.

"None of them worked, none of them, I know it. It's all a waste," spat the magician with frantic mania.

He watched the man, who was obviously illiterate, sit on the edge of his bed and drink the potion. Nothing happened. The man stood up and began to yell profanities about the magician and his credibility.

"Ah! Aggh! He is right. I'm a fool, an idiot. He is right, why do I bother?" groaned the magician to himself right before he blew a deep breath of twinkly dust onto the illiterate man.

The man continued to bash the magician and seemed to come to some realization about what to do about him as he sat down and started to write a letter to the Better Business Bureau. The once illiterate man was furious and sought to show the world what a "hack" the magician was.

"Scoff!" scoffed the magician, riddled with guilt and self-debasement as he staggered to the next customer's house.

The shades were drawn on the bedroom window so the magician passed through the wall and hid behind a chair. In the room, a manish woman sat at her make-up mirror and held the vial. She drank the potion and stared into the mirror as nothing happened. She cried and screamed about the "terrible, terrible" magician and her outrage for believing in such a fraud.

"Another one. Another loss. Another failure. That's all I am, a failure. Why me, why me?" moaned the magician while recoiling and firing laser beams from his eyes which instantly, upon striking the woman, gave her facial hair and toned her upper body into a more muscular build.

Dissatisfied with his purchase, the woman rose from the mirror, went into the bathroom, and urinated standing up. He came out of the bathroom grumbling about how if he ever saw that magician again he'd "kick his ass," and then proceeded to remove his now very loose bra. He sat down and turned on ESPN and grumbled once more about what a "fuckin' cheatin' fraud" he thought the magician to be.

The magician passed back through the wall unnoticed, frantic, and guilt-ridden out into the street. The magician's lips trembled; his eyes were wild, red and teary. He knew they were right; he was a failure. Out he scuttled into the night, bent and broken, knowing he had many more customers left to visit.

3.

THE LITTLE GIRL wanted a red tricycle for Christmas more than anything in the world. Every night before bed, she knelt down and said her prayers and for months leading up to Christmas, she included a request for the red tricycle. The request was always polite and sweet, and with humble dignity she would ask that God would see it fit in his grace and holiness to allow a red tricycle to be found under her Christmas Tree Christmas morning. By the emergence of December, with its singing joy and its festive majesty, the presence of a red tricycle for her and her alone Christmas morning seemed inevitable. It was as if it were already written in the book of life and death, or as if it was commanded by chisel into stone, like the tablets Moses carried in the little girl's Sunday School play where she played his wife, Zipporah.

No one at her church would have denied the little girl's merit in deserving a red tricycle. Nor would either of her parents or her grandparents or her aunts and uncles. The most obvious reason for this was that none of them knew. The little girl told no one, but God and only God alone could have known, for it was to He whom she addressed in her prayers nightly. Not a saint or an angel or even Jesus would do. Integrity in her discipline and her silence held the little girl through her days and her tireless moments in the dark just before sleep, where her little eyes clenched so tight and her lips mumbled their noiseless mantra and her mind wound itself down into oblivion.

She looked at pictures of Saint Theresa on her mother's bedroom wall and thought of all the strength it took to live for God alone. That strength she did not have, she knew, but the little girl held her secret desire as if it was her own cross. The month of December, with its blustery winds and dropping temperature, kept her inside to herself and her vision. She could see Christmas morning, see it clearly before her, with the stockings and the tree and the smell of her mother's cinnamon and brown sugar crepes and the pine and the crackle from her father's small early morning fire. Though she had so few Christmases behind her, she could walk through it all in her mind, all of it down to the biggest box beneath the tree, bearing her name. And the little girl could see herself sitting down to open that present, in its box as big as she, and pulling out her very own red tricycle.

It was the eve of Christmas and the little girl's mother had some last minute shopping to do. Along with her, she brought the little girl to the mall, to look at the snow-white decorations and hear the Yuletide carolers. In the center of the mall, outside the store into which the little girl's mother ventured, was an adorned fountain. Giant snowflakes hung from the ceiling over its bursting shower. Drawn to the waters, and how they played in the air, the little girl lingered outside the store into which her mother ventured. The little girl was captivated by the rhythmic bursts and the way they showered the water's surface and the marble down below. The falling spray twinkled in the mall's track lighting and a sparkle on the nearest bench caught her eye. The golden sparkle was a shiny penny, in top quality although it bore the year of her birth. As her mother called her to join her in the store into which she ventured, the little girl made her one great heartfelt wish for a red tricycle on that shiny penny that bore her birth year and tossed it into the shimmering ripple of the mall fountain.

Christmas morning, the little girl woke with a start; a sleep that took so long to obtain and was very heavy with deep watery dreams trickled away like lost memories gone when she tried to recall. Down the stairs, she treaded lightly and swiftly to the greetings of her parents and the welcome of the whole Christmas panorama. But smells and lights and music and a log fire, along with the advances of her parents, could not derail the little girl from her aim under the tree, where many wrapped gifts glimmered in the blinking lights of the Christmas tree and one stood out above and beyond the others bearing her name. For the sake of discipline, decorum and holiday togetherness, the little girl's parents made her open each gift in an orderly manner giving them a chance to exchange their own. Biding her time to not seem rude and over-anxious, the little girl put the largest present off until the end.

With poise and restrained fervor, the little girl stood up and pulled off the top of the box. All four decorated sides fell to the ground. Inside, on the bottom of the box, sat only a penny. When she picked up the penny, she saw it to be the very same penny from yesterday, all shiny and bearing her birth year, just like it was when she threw it into the mall fountain. Her father knelt down to her and put his arm around her. "I'm sorry, sweetheart," he said to her, "I looked all over town and all the red tricycles were sold out."

ARS MORIENDI (PARABLE FOURTH)

"If there is still one hellish, truly accursed thing in our time, it is our artistic dallying with forms, instead of being like the victims burned at the stake, signaling through the flames."
—Antonin Artaud

IT IS WORSE THAN JUST A GHOST TOWN; even the memories are worn away. They were taken by wind and sun and time. He isn't sure what he is doing here, or even where here is. With the broken buildings behind him, he looks out across the desert to the horizon. He feels like he is standing in a forty-five degree angle made by two lines, the sky a diagonal to the earth; a piece of pie cut out of the Great Nothing. Nevertheless, his resolve to stand in a slice of meaningless space and time with nothing but light, color, and dirt to disguise the abyss is almost soothing.

Turning his back on the distant meeting of the heavens and the earth, he looks at what is left of the town. A gray haze of deteriorating wood buildings lies in front of him. A shoddy group of skeletal remains clustered together as if to shield themselves from the desert, death, and time. The town is a tombstone whose inscription has worn away a long time ago. Walking towards the town it appears to him as an oasis in this desert.

Within the ring of buildings, he surveys the deceased. The

body of the town has decayed with the weight of such time and tempest that no real discerning marks remain. No text, no image. No remnant of human interference is present except for the frail, hollow structures and one day they too will be gone. He stands tall at the center of town, the dry gray shapes leaning in towards him. From his left pocket he draws a pack of Lucky Strike cigarettes and slides one into his mouth. Putting the pack away where it came from, he draws his lighter from his right pant pocket and pauses about mid-chest. He hates smoking, but he has built up the habit in preparation of death. Any moment a shot could ring out or a curtain could fall and he must be ready.

His father died in Mexico, by firing squad, many years ago. He was just a boy but he knew the story well. Growing up he retold himself as a mantra, numbing the brain and stirring the soul. Before they tied his father to the post in the courtyard, they offered him a last cigarette to smoke in his cell. His father requested a Lucky and though hard to obtain, they obliged him out of respect. The last cigarette before death was so cherished that in absolute silence he sat and smoked it, drawing slowly and releasing even slower. As the Lucky burned down with no filter, the sentenced man held on with his fingernails and continued to smoke. After his last long drag, burning his lips, he let the remains go to burn themselves out on descent, landing as nothing but ash and smoke.

He lights the cigarette and clutches at the memory of his father. Standing in the center of town, he tries to take in his surroundings. He wants to know the death it knows. The cigarette hangs from his mouth like a broken branch as his arms slowly extend outwards. He spins slowly to his left, blowing smoke and searching. The speed he spins is slow enough to keep from dizzying, yet fast enough to keep the smoke out of his eyes. The spin is drawn gradually down like a corkscrew into a meditative sitting position with legs crossed. The words trickle from his lips amid streams of smoke:

A Death blow is a life blow to some
Who til they died, did not alive become-
Who had they lived; had died but when
They died, Vitality begun.

The words—so human, so alien—caused a creak amongst the boards that made up this ghost town. The splintering resounded audibly. He first read the poetry of Emily Dickinson in college. Poem number 816 always stood out the most. It made him want to be an artist. So, he studied his history. From Dada, he learned that the only true art is murder and that destruction is the most powerful face of creation. Thus his apprenticeship began.

To kill was easy, he started with bugs and moved up to small mammals. But soon he realized that it wasn't the mere taking of life that made art. The killings he performed were rudimentary and craftsman-like, but there was no art to them. He almost covered the spectrum of species before he understood it wasn't what he did, but how he did it. And as understanding grew, he knew his subject must be human. He also realized that the actual killing became less important than how it must be performed, and the performance must involve totality.

He could not just take a human life; he had to erase a human life. Make a human being, a human life, God's own joy, so it never existed. Many scenarios were planned and many attempts were made only to fail from the limitations of his intellect. The Muse was yet to smile. He was constantly faced with the mystery of human involvement. He fell mesmerized by the endless chain of human connections to other people and to the earth. To take one person's life and wipe that one person's memory and impact from the face of creation he would have to destroy millions of people and square miles of land. The degrees of separation spanned a multitude of links and doubt began to grow of his artistic potential.

Amid a dirty wind, he cries the first tears he has cried since his father's death and continues to smoke with the cigarette sheltered in his cupped hand. The silty wind sticks to his wet face and his tears become like quicksand, pulling him down further. The ghost town is no longer still; a torrent is mounting—fierce, primal, and invisible. He remembers how he got here. He remembers his son and his last chance at artistry. A year ago he came across a virgin runaway and the Muse finally smiled. They moved out to the desert and he soon impregnated her. For nine months they lived alone and no one knew she was pregnant. Fortuitously, she died during childbirth as he delivered the baby out of doors with minimal medical skills. He wrapped the baby in only one blanket and placed the baby on only one table. No one was around to hear the baby cry. He then built a great fire and was careful to burn the mother's whole body, leaving no sign of pregnancy. Next the table, blanket, and baby were all burned.

It took the whole night to burn out every facet of his creative process, stoking the flames and grinding down the ashes into dust and then air, but he felt a satisfaction in suffering for his art. He now truly felt himself an artist. He had thought of everything. Nothing in the world bore any sign of his son's existence, no name, no trace. Complete destruction of a human life, wiped away like a sandcastle into the sea. The art of death, of true totality in destruction, is achieved. A person, a life existed, and is now gone and no one knows. No one except him, of course. The realization broke his consciousness with the dawn and satisfaction was replaced by a fit of rage. The rage was brief though and followed by empty resolution as he walked out into the desert.

His walk brought him many miles, and finally to this ghost

town. He would have to die for his creation to live. He would have to die to be an artist. The sandstorm dissipated and the ghost town exhaled its resuscitated breath only to remain empty and dead again. He remains still, sitting, trying like hell to savor his cigarette. There is no sound.

Many artists experience fame posthumously. There is always something left until there isn't, he thinks, as he looks out to the horizon where it seems the heavens are getting closer to the earth. The forty-five degree angle is getting smaller. His art is of a fourth dimension. Space ends with time.

SOMETHING THAT HAPPENED A LONG TIME AGO

FROM 'THE FISH FAMILY ALBUM'

STEW's FATHER spent most nights sitting at the computer in his bedroom online, often in Catholic chat rooms. Stew's parents slept in separate rooms. It had been this way for many years. Once when Stew asked his mother the reason for this, she told him to ask his father. His father said that his mother snored and as a result he lost sleep. So they slept in separate rooms. His mother didn't really sleep much anyway. She stayed up in the living room pretty late each night watching television and smoking cigarettes. Stew's father did not smoke. He did not do much of anything for all I knew. When I would stop by to see Stew in the evening, his father was always back there in the bedroom. I would talk to his mother, though. She was very nice and I would try to be very polite. Mrs. Fish would always offer over the remote control to us to see if there was anything we would rather watch on television.

The times that I saw both of Stew's parents together seemed very awkward. Maybe I just felt awkward since it was an unfamiliar situation. I never saw them touch. I spent more time with Mrs. Fish than her husband, but I would see him on occasion when we passed by his bedroom door on the way to Stew's room. The door would always be cracked just enough for him to see us pass. Sometimes he would ask me questions since he knew I was also Catholic. One time, to break a tense silence, I told him that my father taught me some theology and he dismissed what I said by saying he preferred dogma to theology. I was always a little scared of these conversations since I once made a joke about Catholic guilt and he made an angry and shamed face and turned around in his seat back to the computer without saying anything more to me.

Mrs. Fish was still a Baptist. She didn't convert when her husband did. Stew didn't really care either way and his parents never really said much about such things to him. His little brother went to mass with his father on Sundays. Stew often slept at my house on Saturday nights. He said his mother never went with them to mass, but always seemed a little upset left at home.

One day when Stew and I were hanging out in his basement, his father called down for Stew to come up. I sat there alone while Stew went up. Shortly he came back down with a poster in his hands. Stew showed me the art print and I saw it to be a Georgia O'Keefe. One of her enlarged flower cross-sections. This one was an orchid. It had mauves and lavenders in it with a high concentration of pink around its center. The labial quality of cross-sectioned petals was undeniable. The dark depth in the middle, surrounded by the pink added to the undeniably vaginal quality of the whole painting. Stew said his father asked him if he would like to have it. To which Stew answered, yes. When he asked his father why he was getting rid of it he only answered, before turning around in his chair back to his computer, "It reminds me of something that happened a long time ago, that I don't want to think about anymore."

DR. MAME

PSEUDOCEROS BIFURCUS

DR. MAME removes her glasses and rubs her eyes, kneading the dry dough-like skin. The nights seemed to be getting later. The coffee didn't stay warm enough long enough, the metal stools hurt her butt and lower back, and the lab tables were always cold on her forearms as she leaned over her work. How far it is she has come. At last, she finished her doctorate. She got a good job at this lab and finally after two years of putting in seventy-hour weeks she was promoted to Director. What has it got her? She's pushing thirty and her life is graphs, charts, and pages of data, and of mostly other people's research at that. The esteemed Dr. Mame never gets to go on site, she never gets to go out in the boat, and she hardly ever gets to spend any time in the tanks even. And this is her work, this is what's supposed to matter most. Sure, she got that promotion and this job and the doctorate, but at what cost? The notion of a social life has always been inconceivable, yet as was said before, she is pushing thirty.

She hated to think that that could be the missing link to her happiness. Still the notion grew and she in turn entered deeper into her work. That's probably how she got this last promotion to Director. A little over a year ago her sister got pregnant and married and Dr. Mame worked like a beast unchained for about nine months. About the time her fury subsided her awed superiors, amazed at her fetish for menial lab work, promoted her to Director of the whole lab. With a whole lab under her reign she has more work, more supposed esteem, and more listless yearning, which of course she hasn't the time to notice.

"Hey Mamey, I mean Dr. Mame, where would you like these specimens?"

"Over on that table is fine, Georg."

Oh Georg. Georg was one of the original perks of the promotion. A six foot three blonde Norwegian interning some lab time while pursuing his Masters. His strong toned physique bronzed by the alien sun of an alien shore was keen for application. Gyorg, at hand and foot, always ready to lend a hand where a hand was needed, always brought a smile to Dr. Mame's face, but recently even that was waning. His persistent readiness, once a flattering and appetizing part of a day's work, has now become a pestering annoyance. Even his little nickname for her, Mamey, at first cute and endearing, eventually became the topic of a little reprimanding talk she entertained her staff with, clarifying the finer points of respect and protocol.

Yes, she still can see how attractive Georg is, and God only knows how long ago her last date was, but all the excitement has gone out of the prospect. Georg is just the guy who carries in and unloads the orders and specimens for her and can possibly, if need be, run errands. Just another part of her staff that she has to over see and direct.

"That's all of them. Do you need anything else, Dr. Mame?"

"No, no thank you, that'll be all Georg."

The hard work was all definitely worth it, but she was just beginning to feel so tired. Moreover, she was plagued by that cliché about regulations on rest for the weary. The mere thought of rest made her get up and busy herself with work. At hand were the new specimens and they could provide a working distraction far superior to reviewing pages of data from other people's work.

She begins by preparing the specimens for observation and looking over their charts. It seems the lab had just received samples of a marine flatworm called Pseudoceros bifurcus. As she observes, Dr. Mame notes their activity with a raised eyebrow and a curious and thoughtful "humpf". She is confused as to what the pairs of worms are doing but enthralled in watching the process. The way they move at each other and dodge, rear and spring, like a violent dance, draws the flushed doctor farther into this work-related divergence and drives her blood hotter. With blood mounting in her once pallid cheeks, the same blood that was roused to finish the doctorate, get this job, and the promotion to director, she checks the charts and reads that the worms are hermaphroditic and the activity she watches is a form of penis fencing where the slower weaker worm, defeated and stabbed by the penis of the competitor, is inseminated and forced to carry the child of the pair. Apparently, in hermaphroditic organisms, the desire to inseminate is as strong as the desire not to be inseminated. Once these creatures begin to resist the passivity and submission of child bearing they must keep fighting, always avoiding the penises and desires of others and always stabbing when the chance is given, doing whatever it takes to stay at the same fast, safe, and triumphant pace of life they have always fought for. Once they get you down you're out.

After reading, Dr. Mame watches a little more of the flatworms and their violent dance. She smiles sadly at the bittersweet victories of the fastest worm and a love she will never know. Placing her glasses on the lab table and rubbing her hard red eyes, she rises with a deep authoritative yawn that still squeaks at its peak. Dr. Mame is very tired and decides that she deserves to go home early—she was the director wasn't she— and have a long overdue rest.

BREAK THE SKIN

"Did you?…"

"…Oh, you did."

"What are you doing?"

"I'm just looking at it, checking you out. Does it hurt?"

"It feels okay, a little sore."

"I'll kiss it and make it better. Now I'll blow on it…there… ooh, I can see inside you."

"No, oh, don't look at it."

"But it's cute. You're beautiful."

"You're so weird, how can you say that?"

"I love every inch of your body."

"But how can you when it's all open like that? I can't even look at it."

"Wuss."

"Ugh…Anyway, I can't believe I'm this comfortable with you. I can't believe I'm letting you do this. Why are you so interested?"

"I don't know, it's just that sense of awe and wonder and mystery, ya know. Not to wax trite and all psycho-sensual, or get too over-analytical, but it's like looking into my own mortality."

"Oh stop!"

"No, it's just that here I can see weakness and strength at once. I came out of a body just like this one."

"Thanks, that's an image."

"No, I mean, I love you, and here I see your vulnerability and I want to be inside you."

"We've done that already."

"Yeah, I know, but I really want to be inside you, like crawling into your wound and healing you, sealing you, complete and enclosed with me inside."

"Oh Sweety, but am I really that wounded?"

"No, but the cut is deep."

"Should we get a Band-Aid?"

"No, I think it'll close on its own, I'll blow on it more."

"Gently."

"Sorry. Here. Like this?"

"Yes, that's nice."

"It kind of looks like a socket missing an eye."

"What?"

"The elliptical shape and its depth."

"Oow, you sure know how to talk to a girl."

"No...I'm sorry, but I was just thinking—if eyes are the windows to the soul, then there is nothing here to impair me looking into your soul and I feel I want to be inside you again."

"I'd like you inside of me...you're sweet."

"Thank you."

"Kiss it again, then let's let it rest and heal."

"Okay. There."

FATHER, SON, AND HOLY GHOST

FROM 'THE PIT, AND NO OTHER STORIES'

SHANGHAI, NOVEMBER 1945—The pain came again with the falling rain. Throbbing, a dull ache. Each step in each murky puddle, pain. More weight on the left foot, the right just the heel. Across the square he hobbles. No one cares to notice. Everyone is running in the rain. They run until the square is empty. He swings his right leg, bounding light off the heel, little pressure. The rain is thick in overlapping grids. His skin grows wet through his coat. Rising puddles touch his left toes cold. That one boot, far more worn than the other. There is no light, no stars, no moon. There is no sound but rain.

Swei Li Quok halts his breath. He is listening. In the shelter of the overhang, he has a moment to pause. A wall of sound becomes no sound. He breathes. Crossing the square seemed once impossible. Now he looks ahead even further. The pain is where his right toes once were. He calls them his Phantom Barometers. He felt the rain thirty minutes before it fell. He looks down at the right boot. It is stuffed with a rag and tight to the water. Quok concentrates and wiggles nothing.

The wall is red. Around the corner, he sees nothing. He looks again. No light, only rain. He pivots back on his right heel. The heel is numb and strong. Eight years to callous. One bullet for five toes. His life for cowardice. Quok waits, looks, and listens. It is impossible to hear footfall in this rain. It is impossible to see with no moon. Still, Quok waits for his mark, waiting for movement through the rain. He thinks of eight years of cowardice, eight years without honor. For a clean up sweep the soldiers returned. Quok played dead. Beneath his father and his friends he lay still and silent. He held his breath and held his tears. The soldiers spread blanket fire. Through the body of Quok's father one bullet reached his right foot. In the heat of August he lay, his sweat and their blood moving together. With night, Quok stole away. He was still in the hospital in December. It was there he heard the news. 80,000 Japanese soldiers in Nanking: his mother one of 20,000 women systematically raped; his brothers of the 200,000 killed.

From a door a man will come. In this direction he will walk. Quok will strike out from under his coat. He will stab the man in the abdomen and clutch the man to silence him. The man will fall dead in the street, dead in the rain. This is what Quok tells himself. He is doing this for China, for the Revolution. It is also for his family and his father. The man for whom he waits is not Japanese but still he will kill for his family. Eight years, alone with his cowardice. Alone while the world warred and to him it was nothing. The war has ended but not to China. In his lifetime, Swei Li Quok's father heard his son deny the Revolution. The Japanese came and Japanese went and now Swei Li Quok understands the Revolution.

Quok's father once stood here. Not geographic location, but thematic location. 1927 Peking, at a street corner, Quok's father stood. His eyes were across on a dark window. Sir John Waltzingcock walked down the lobby of the British Embassy. To his secretary, Ms. Pool, he said he was off to lunch. Jenny Kwan, translator and file clerk, was at the East window. Sir Waltzingcock directed his eyes to her ass. It was round in a modest black skirt. Jenny Kwan smiled over her right shoulder at the Lord and pulled the cord of the closed drapes. The light of the eastern sun filled the room, interrupting his gaze. Jenny Kwan continued to smile, Quok's father had his signal, and Sir Waltzingcock walked out the door. Two minutes later Waltzingcock lay dead in the street. Quok's father was gone.

Now Swei Li Quok must be his father's son. There is no one left. He pulls the dagger from his pocket. The dagger is dark in the shadow of his coat. Quok's eyes are used to the dark. He said he would do anything to help. They told him this would help. They had a tip. Across the street distant light is shadowed in the rain. The shadow takes a form and the form approaches. Quok crouches low, pivoting on his right heel. He holds his breath. The form is gyrating as it moves. This is the man, his mark. They told him the mark was a Spasmodic Type. Quok exhales shortly and holds another breath. His right foot goes forward first. From it Quok steps with his left. The balance remaining on his right foot falls early off the missing toes. Swei Li Quok stumbles as he lunges at the form before him in the rain.

A NIGHT,
LIKE ANY OTHER
OR
OOH, OOH THAT SMELL

GASOLINE IS POURED on the dead face. The body, entirely saturated. Drying blood charges with the illusion of new life as the gas sweeps across the body. There is a match, torn from its book with two trembling fingers, struck and placed. It lands on the chest, a ring of blue bursting magically forth around it, like a ripple from a pebble in a still pond. And there is a flame—five feet eleven inches head to toe, a wall of seething heat, arching and whipping high into the already humid Georgia night. There is a smoke—stirred and swollen, grand and dirty, thick and pungent. And there is a smell—gas fire, then singed cloth and hair, then putrid bitter bite of burnt flesh. Open eyes, stung red with smoke from red flesh and flame. A gray smoke plays among yellow teeth as a smile slowly and wickedly forms. His scrotum tightens up to match his anxious stomach. Bathed with satisfaction, in the scarring air, fostering memory, Jimmy Red walks back to his mother's truck. It is a night unlike any other.

※

A DOOR STANDS with one side bearing a stolen metal "No

Trespassing" sign facing out to the main hall of a small two-bedroom ranch-style house while the other side, bearing a Baywatch poster of three swim-suited women, faces in on Jimmy. Naked from the waist down, he holds his penis in his left hand. Young Master Red uses his right hand to slowly turn the pages of a magazine, from back to front.

"Jimmy, you home?"

"Yup, Mah."

The left hand loses its grip on its shrinking prisoner. A wet tongue searches a dry mouth. A loose tooth. The tongue pushes the tooth in a slow grinding groove as Jimmy bites his lip.

"Where were you last night, Jimmy?"

"Out drivin', you know how I like to drive, Mah."

"Are you alright? You didn't hit a skunk or anything did you?"

"Nah."

"There some clothes soaking in the sink. You want me to wash 'em?"

"I put 'em to soak last night. Jus' leave it."

"If they been soakin' all night, how come they still smell so bad? What happened anyway?"

"Shit, mah! I've got it. Just stop now. I'm trying to rest."

"Did you go to school today?"

"SHIT, MAH!"

Through the door Jimmy is heard to tremble, yet still she walks away.

✻

JIMMY'S FATHER was a pig trucker. "Big Red's Hog Haulin'" read the sign on the truck. He hauled swine all over the southeast. When Jimmy was eleven years old, his father steered a load of pigs towards Kentucky and never came back. Over the last five years Jimmy hasn't eaten pork once.

⁕

7:30 BROUGHT MANY SOUNDS: Wheel of Fortune on the TV; the sigh of the recliner giving of itself to support a tired woman's large weight; the opening of Jimmy's window so he wouldn't have to see her as he left. He denied her dinner already and he knew she would leave him alone.

Down at the Citgo station, the regular group of kids mulled about. Jimmy passed about them slowly, stiffly. His baseball hat, low, shadowed his twittering, flittering eyes. Darryl was the first to notice the smell.

"Shit, Jimmy, you been bathin' in your barbecue again? You smell like burnt meat, boy. Gawd Damn!" That was Darryl.

Like rats, they circled in. The smell was thick enough to attract the whole crowd. The ridicule was easy and the weakness was pungent. Darryl wasn't the biggest. Lennrd was the biggest, his size saved him from the difficulties of the missing vowel, and he naturally assumed his place directly in front of Jimmy.

"So Bastard Jimmy is now Stinky Bastard Jimmy." Awkward laughter. Lennrd is always right. If Jimmy is uncool, Lennrd let them know, and they should act accordingly.

"I ain't no bastard." He seemed to spit a little as he spoke.

"Then where's your daddy, bastard?" The crowd waits with a secret fearful joy.

"He's out haulin' pigs, tha's all." The lie came out like a whimper.

"He should be at home haulin' that pig of a mother of yours." Lennrd peppered his words with a poke of the pelvis. The crowd let loose. The pelvis kept poking as the face made pig snorts. Fist clenched, face red, Jimmy's eyes swelled. He stammered. He spit. Lennrd punched him in the face. Jimmy went down with blood on his lip and another loose tooth. The space around Jimmy became denser. Eyes widened. Kicks connected with his ribs and face-defending forearms.

"What are you gonna do Stinky Bastard? You gonna cry again, huh, Stinky Bastard?" And the kicks kept coming.

✳

HIS RIGHT T-SHIRT SLEEVE thickened and stiffened as more snot, blood, and tears were wiped on it. Both sleeves were beginning to have the rough guilty texture his shorts have when he wakes up from those "dirty, dirty dreams," as his mother calls them. Jimmy sat on the steps to the back door of his dark, quiet house. He wished there were somewhere else to go and slowly rubbed his sore gums through his cheek, staring hard at the dense wall of Georgia pine trees that trapped his view.

A sloppy, old golden retriever loped from the left to the right of Jimmy's field of vision home to the next door neighbor's house.

"Sandy! Here girl! Sandy!" went Jimmy's desperate pleas as the dog eyed him sideways and hurried her heavy trudge home.

"She mus' smell that mighty smoke on me, jus' like all of them. They don't un'erstan' I earned it an' I'd do it again." Jimmy spoke out loud to himself.

"I'd burn you too, you…you…you bitch-dog." As he stuttered, he lifted a handful of rocks and released them like a spreading buckshot all about the now distant dog who trotted and whimpered, but did not look back, familiar with the ways of man.

Jimmy cried for the third time today. The first was before masturbating in the afternoon, and the second during his Citgo confrontation with his peers.

"If they only knew. If they only knew what I could do." Through the tears, Jimmy began to soliloquize. "I'd show 'em. Yes, I would. If only they knew. There is someone who knows. Oh yes. But he ain't talkin', no he ain't, but boy does he know. He ain't got nothin' left to talk with, I saw to that." The tears fell away. "Shit. If only they'd see him jus' like they smelled him they'd be damn sick with knowing. They'll find out though. It's got to be on the news or somethin' soon. They'll see it on the news and they'll remember my smell and it'll be clear who to watch out for." He rose and began to pace. "An' they'll be scared of me an' of what I might do to 'em. They'll know their noses were right. An' they won't go thinkin' I'm no bastard no more 'cause I ain't no bastard an' I'll burn any body that say so." He was really hot now. "I might not start shit, but I finish it. Anyone can start somethin' and leave but not everyone has what it takes to finish shit, like I do. Jus' like I finished that one last night. I sure finished him. Who knows who started him that way, but they left and I sure finished him. Some other might do the killing, but I do the burning, I do the finishin'. Yep, and I'll finish them all too, those bastards." He was getting louder and louder. "They're bastards, them. I ain't no bastard. I ain't no BASTARD!"

A light came on in his house and Jimmy could hear his mother call his name while at the same time the forgetful golden retriever came bobbing back as if bastard was its trained summons.

"Jimmy!" His mother called again, as he hit the dog with a rock just below her left eye, causing her to wink, yelp, and turn away, forgetful no longer. The dog, homeward bound and pitiful again, was almost struck by another spite-charged stone when Jimmy's mother came to the window.

"Jimmy what the hell are you doin'? You have school tomorrow. Get your butt in bed right this minute!"

"Shit, Mah!" Jimmy asserted, and yet went straight into the house to bed.

GRISTLE,
OR WHAT IS LEFT

"'Forgive me, but I don't believe you,' Woland replied,
'that cannot be: manuscripts do not burn.'"

—Bulgakov, *Master and Margarita*, pg. 287

WHEN I WAS MUCH YOUNGER and trying to be a writer, I wrote
my first book titled, *Gristle, or What is Left.* It was about the night
adventures of a very confused and very zealous young man. The
young man was in college at the time and trying to write, but had
nothing to write about. All of this changed when he first read
Henry Miller's *Tropic of Cancer.* He learned that all that mattered
was to live and to write. To write and to live. Like I, the young man
happened to be in a small bookstore one day in Bronxville, a store
that must have usually serviced Sarah Lawrence students, which
we weren't. Standing there among a couple of friends, the book,
Tropic of Cancer, was lifted off the rack. The name was familiar,
both the book and the author, maybe from the movie "Henry and
June." The friends walked on and we read the back of the book.
*The other side of Paris in the 20's...far from the glitz and literary
culture of Hemingway, Fitzgerald, and the Lost Generation...the
slums where a different kind of writing emerged from a different kind
of expatriate...* is about what it said, from what I can remember.

The young man bought the book and showed it to his

friends. He said something like, "Sally, Andy, I've heard of this guy, and always wanted to check him out and had no idea what it would be like. Seems like it is a darker, more sexual, seedy side of the Lost Generation." He knew Sally liked those guys too, but growing up at the end of the 20th century and not the beginning, would also prefer a more sexual seedy version.

The young man started reading the book as they left the store and walked around Bronxville. And that night during dinner. And after dinner. And the next day; but stopped somewhere before the end. He had all he needed. He needed to know what could be done and here it was. He was free. He had a writing assignment, a semester to write a novella and now he had learned how from Henry Miller.

In pursuit of life, writing fodder, and the life of a writer, he plotted a specific path for the rest of the semester. The young man moved into a world of night adventures. College was perfect for this. One thousand students, all contained in a safe and secure environment, and all on different schedules for classes. This meant that safely on campus at night there would always be someone to talk to, hang out with, drink with, *live* with. Gradually, as he moved into a more nocturnal sleeping and waking schedule, some things had to give way. He couldn't make it to his morning classes and only his latest in the day became in any way convenient and therefore more amusing to attend. Soon enough he had to break up with his girlfriend, for not only did it not fit his sleep schedule, but she stood in the way of most of the more writerly of Henry Miller-esque adventures, and ultimately the breakup provided great drama for great prose and introspection and more great prose.

After all, that's why he did this, for the writing. Between four and seven most mornings he would make it back to his dorm room—sometimes a little earlier—and commence his writing for the night. Often drunk and always wired, as this new path in life brought a great deal of zeal out of him, he wrote. "I'm doing it, I'm a writer, I really am," he thought deep down. Every night that zeal carried him through the drunkenness to put down words to the page, chronicling the night, ranting through his feelings about his actions and the people he experienced. He cited philosophers, made literary references, and felt brilliant and real. He named the book, *Gristle, or What is Left*, from a quote by a friend he dearly loved and respected.

The previous semester, during Thanksgiving break, he and David sat in a diner in Atlanta drinking coffee and chain-smoking. The first time he met David, years before, David explained to the young man that he once got himself addicted to morphine just to see what it felt like to get withdrawals and kick. David introduced the young man to the work of William S. Burroughs. They were in the diner because the young man was starting his own Literary Magazine at his college and he wanted to feature David.

The scene in the diner is the young man interviewing David for quotes. The room was dank and smoky, as the smoking section was tucked back in the corner near the door to the kitchen's dish pit. The neverending pot of coffee gave out lukewarm coffee to the boys.

"I just want some quotes," the young man said. "Whatever you want to give. Pearls of wisdom, witty quips, whatever. My readers might not be ready for it, but they need it."

"Alright, here you go: 'hors d'oeuvres is a hard word to spell,'" David said matter-of-factly. He was trying to make his joke stronger by not laughing at it himself as the young man struggled to write it down and spell the French.

He rambled out a couple more and the young man recognized at least one to be a rip-off of, or homage to, Burroughs. The food came, burgers, and they took a break. When they were done, the young man buggered a couple more out of David and he ended by saying, "Gristle is the only thing worth remembering."

The young man remembered this powerful line soon after beginning his night adventures. He got out the first issue of the Postmodernist Modernist Post and sat pondering the quote. He plugged Gristle in as the title of the book and gave up pages and pages to dissecting what Gristle meant as a word very late one night. He had just come home from some crazy spin the bottle party where he saw twin sisters kiss (both of whom he kissed too). It was after all the dissecting of the word that night that he also added the subtitle, what is left.

By the end of Spring Break, after some time alone, he couldn't do it any more. He was tired, he had alienated some friends, he was worried about how many sexual partners he now had, his grades had slipped almost beyond repair, and he missed his girlfriend. Maybe she could save him. Maybe that was the kind of story he was living and writing. He was a romantic, that could not be denied. So he won her back. He always knew he could do it. This came with certain conditions though. He had to hide his book, no *Gristle* for anyone but his writing professor. Also, he had to avoid all the people he associated with during his night adventures, which led to new feelings of alienation. He had her though, she would keep him safe. Redeem himself in her eyes and her love would protect him. Henry Miller was a romantic too.

Eventually, the benefits of an insular, safe campus with a student body of one thousand proved detrimental and his girlfriend began to experience first hand and through hearsay the reality of his night adventures. He cried and clung so hard to her, purgating himself and waiting out the clock and calendar until summer. The zeal and seedy venom that characterized *Gristle*, distilled from the night adventures soon corrupted everything. His writing professor had liked the earliest chapters, but here at the end, the only opportunity to make his life and all he had done to it mean anything was denied. She hated it. They sat there in the school's café at a scheduled meeting. The young man had left the novella in her mailbox a week ago and hoped and prayed since then until now that he would have justification. If his girlfriend found out everything from his night adventures, it couldn't hurt him if he was a real writer.

The professor was waiting when he got there and he sat down and put on a smile. "So, what do you think?" he asked. He tried to sound and act chipper, trying to make reality a reflection of himself.

She tried to sound calm when she started with "There are some problems here," but he couldn't help but detect some anger in her tone. She went on to say many things he tried not to hear or remember, but the worst and final stood out: "Disrespectful to the art of narrative," she said.

That was it for the young man. He said, "okay, I'll fix it," and left without meaning what he said or looking her in the eyes.

That was it. The semester was almost over and he found a ride home to Atlanta from a friend on her way to Florida. The catch, which was no catch for him, was that she was leaving early. Maybe he finally caught a break. It was a free ride, was his excuse to his girlfriend, for leaving early. And that was it. He did not fix *Gristle* or turn it in. He didn't finish his classes. He just left.

They left in the rain and when they reached Baltimore after four hours, the skies were blue and he sighed, expelling so much air that he had made it, he had gotten away. Straight through to Atlanta, fourteen hours, and they slept together in his bed. He was gone and the past couldn't touch him. The next day his friend left and he went about a very different life. The college stories were funny or glorious in the retelling to his home friends. They understood him. Eventually, he let a couple of guys read *Gristle* and they liked it. He told them what the professor had said, "Disrespectful to the art of narrative," and the consensus was that from a writing teacher at an institution, he should take it as a compliment. They agreed that the Art of Narrative was a hard thing to disrespect.

After a month of occasional phone calls, the young man broke up with his girlfriend again through a letter. It was very literary and even said they were not destined to be together "because they were ideologically opposed." They never spoke again and he never went back to that college.

He hung onto *Gristle* for six months in Atlanta before tearing up the one typed copy and putting it in a brown paper bag. He then burned the bag. A year after that, he told the whole story to David and reminded him of where the title came from. He didn't remember.

"Remember, you were giving me quotes for the Postmodernist Modernist Post and you said 'Gristle is the only thing worth remembering.'" He didn't seem to remember still, and then it was perfectly clear.

"Nooooo, I said, 'Gristle is the only *word* worth remembering'"

To this, the young man said: "Okay, that must be it, I wrote it down wrong. What is the difference anyway, between, 'Gristle is the only *thing* worth remembering,' and 'Gristle is the only *word* worth remembering?' What did you mean?"

"I don't know what the difference is. I just remember it was *word*, not *thing*. I was probably ripping off or quoting something; I don't remember."

WINTER SOLSTICE

IN THE FRONT YARD, there is a nativity scene that awaits the birth of its Christ. Mother set up the display about two weeks ago. Father and she used to do it together. The first weekend of December they would go up in the attic on Sunday afternoon and bring down all of the supplies. Out they would go, into the winter twilight, and there they would set up all the parts to the plastic set. I would watch from inside, with my face pressed up against the glass of the bay window, cold but curious. First, Father would drive in the poles and place the roof of the manger lean-to. Mother would stand the three wise men, bearing their fake plastic gifts, to the right of the opening while Father spread hay from a bail he picked up on his way home from work. The cradle was then placed by Mother, and Father flanked it with the hollow plastic shells representing Mary and Joseph. Together they would ceremoniously lay the Baby Jesus doll to rest as if his rubber skin needed their soft care. This year she did it all alone. Since I am the man of the house now, after Father's death, I guess I could have helped, but I never helped before.

As a child, I watched the ritual with awe and reverence, a little too much reverence to ever participate, since fear I have always felt in reverence. Even as a rebellious teenager my eyes would be on the pair of them out there, like a King and Queen placing their very own child on a throne in the chill dusky air, and I could not help but respect them. With the respect was always a little fear, too.

Father used to tell me that Jesus was not really born on December 25th. He would say that it was really a celebration of the Winter Solstice, or Saturnalia, for the ancient Romans. Actually, most cultures had some form of seasonal holiday at this time. Jesus was most likely born in spring—near Passover, maybe around April—was the consensus he said most scholars had. His eyes would shift and he would lower his voice, as if he was scared someone was listening, when he would tell me that the Church assimilated this holiday and made it their most holy to appease the pagans they sought to convert. It was all politics, all propaganda. When I asked Father why he went through it all, why the nativity scene, why all the care, he would answer that he did it all for her, for Mother.

Before I was old enough to understand what all of this meant, I sometimes felt a little ashamed when I would see his zeal out there in construction of the scene. To celebrate Jesus' birthday when he knew it was not, just for her, for love. But, he said there were other reasons to celebrate. Father told me that the beauty of this holiday for the pagans was that, though it looked and felt like a time of death and despair, it held the promise of rebirth and renewal. Although the ground was cold, seeds were planted to grow at a later time; they gestated there, in the belly of the earth, just below the surface. He pointed out that our Christmas tree was an evergreen and represented the continuity of life. I tried to understand that there was something more in it for him.

Last year, Father went into the hospital the first week of December. He had a stroke in his sleep. I came home early from school for the holidays. Mother and I spent his last few weeks in the hospital with him. I would watch through the glass in the intensive care unit as Mother sat by Father and held his unresponsive hand, limp and rubbery. There was no nativity last year. Instead of Christmas, we had a wake.

I went back to school as soon as I could and did not return until this holiday break. I spent the summer in the dorms, avoiding Mother. I even tried to dodge her telephone calls as best as I could, but she left messages and her letters piled up. For the last two weeks I have spent most of my time sitting here, in this bay window box, in this quiet and shadowy house looking at the back of the nativity scene on the lawn, in the same place where I watched her set it up alone, the same place where I watched them both set it up for the last time two years ago. Mother and I have not spoken much since I have been home.

I was quiet last night as I waited outside of her door. When her light went out I knew she wasn't asleep, but I listened a while longer in silence. Silence was all that came back at me from her room. She did not sleep much anymore, but I hoped her motionless attention was elsewhere so she wouldn't know what I was doing. After ample time, I crept outside, careful of the front door's hum, almost like a voice in the dead winter house. Over the hard earth of the lawn, I made my way to the nativity scene. As I approached, I felt the six plastic wise man eyes upon me, an intruder in their midst, not part of their tradition. My pulse pounded in their presence, I felt alive, and they were stiff and powerless to my sense of purpose. Mary and Joseph looked at me too, hollow shells they were, plastic, empty. But Baby Jesus glowed there wrapped up in his cradle, not like the others. With precision and quick care, I swooped up the Baby Jesus and held him to my breast. Without thinking, but knowing exactly what I was doing, I was on my knees, instantly digging. The only image in my mind was of the squirrels on the quad at my college. Only a month ago I witnessed their calculated winter plans where they hid acorns and nuts in the ground so that after the snow sets in and the trees are bare, there is food that lies beneath the cold. I remember wondering how many acorns are never found and though a squirrel might go hungry, an oak has the chance to grow.

So now, I look out to the back of the nativity scene and listen to find out if Mother has gone to bed. There is a shadow of the five forms cast onto the frosted lawn by the streetlight. The three wise men are to the left and the two parents to the right, still in the cold night. I cannot see where the earth was overturned last night, where it was stamped down with my boot, and where the Baby Jesus now rests, but I look out and wait for spring and the warmth that it will bring.

AUGUSTUS AND ANASTASIA

FROM 'THE ROAD KILLS'

"For Thy mercy, O Lord, is in the heavens, and Thy truth reacheth unto the clouds. The clouds pass away but the heaven abideth."

—St. Augustine, *Confessions*

I'M DRIVING NORTH on the highway, driving home. In the air, I can smell the rain that has yet to fall. Trees cling tight to old gentle hills in preparation and thirst. The horizon is timber wolf gray. The upper sky is thick and dense. It is almost upon me. Charcoal in color, it has bubbles and clumps that move in such congestion they still hold the form. Into the timber wolf horizon dip vicious stalactites, gnarly sugared teeth, gloomy wagging shriveled teats. I drive under these clouds and their foreboding. I ride between the road and the timber wolf and the charcoal closes and threatens, piercing the still horizon. These clouds, I like to watch. From a distance I can observe them, their movements, their startling darkness. But I don't want to get too close. I don't want to feel them. I don't want to experience them. Someone else should. He should. They are meant for him.

Rain breaks down in mounting sheets, each beat thicker than the last. A building is felt as Augustus drives north. His head swims in the rain. It rises up from the road to meet the downfall and he is somewhere in between. Swimming forward against the road-water kickback of faster cars. The windshield wipers fight hard and he sees between their efforts. They cause a dirt-water runoff that drips in through his cracked window. Every time he ashes his cigarette, the tawny drops catch his hand. Now, at least, this does not bother him.

Augustus met Anastasia two weeks ago. It was three days before the end of school. Three days before she went home for the summer. Home, an hour and half away. At the time he had yet to find a home.

Upon meeting, on that Wednesday, when she was accompanying a mutual friend in pursuit of a video, they relaxed into rambled scattered conversation bits. She looked at his compact discs and his books and finally she borrowed a film. Mutual interests abounded. They both have saints' names and they enjoyed that. Cut from the same spirit of faith, he waxed at the time. They even had the same birth signs. The next day, they talked once in his room after she had stopped by. For their second meeting, that very day they spent a couple of hours outside the library, talking and smoking till three in the morning. That time he had stopped by and she let him occupy her study time.

It was outside of the library that he asked her to a movie for her last night at school. With her answer being yes, energized over a mutual film selection, Augustus went home smiling. In bed, he thought of her. His heart beat hard with nicotine and zeal. He tried not to plan, and he fought not to think too much. So he cataloged all that she had said. By the time sleep came upon him, Augustus' mind was dizzy with smoke and coincidence.

Friday he told many friends about her. He has told many more since. All marvel at the odds. Even now, as it was then, he will not let anyone use the word perfect. Perfection would always infer heartbreak, because how can anyone be perfect? Where is the let down? He still wonders now what fear of perfection infers.

Being her last day, she had to spend time with her two roommates. They went along to the movie. He paid for everyone; it was the only way he could smoothly pay for her. Anastasia rode in the passenger seat of his car. Other than the occasional word dropped into the back seat, Augustus and Anastasia were in their own world. During the movie they whispered together, laughed together, and felt together. After, they drove back with garrulous exuberance in their front seat world of continuous stories and cigarettes.

In the parking lot of school, he asked her why she couldn't just leave in the morning. She told him that someone was expecting her. She was to leave immediately and go straight from his car to her car. Nevertheless, they talked a little by her car. Anastasia handed him a piece of paper, folded. It held her name, address, telephone number, and e-mail address already written out for him. Augustus smiled to himself, for he was still unsure how to ask for such things. They made tentative plans for him to call her and for them to hang out in the next week. Then she hugged him and he hugged back and still she hugged and it was tight and he felt her against him and he could swear he felt *something*. It was as *real* as a hug could be and still just be a hug.

Her right arm and then hand lingered down his left arm as the hug separated. He thinks he pulled away first, though he can't think of why. They said goodbye and she got in her car. He walked away, towards the dorm, lighting a cigarette. Just before the building, he turned, almost coy-like, and he looked to her car at the stop sign. He wondered if she lingered to look back at him, as he was then doing to her. Augustus waved and Anastasia waved back.

In the torrent, Augustus smokes hard and the car takes on that sticky smell of damp smoke. Looking hard through rain driven to the earth and rain repelled by it, he is still going north, still swimming in his thoughts of her, and still getting wet on his left arm by downpour created by his own wipers. The drops on his left arm make him wonder, if he tried hard enough, could he feel them as her hand or even fingertips trailing down those same places, as if coming out of that hug. Augustus tries and can barely crack a smile at his silliness. Nowhere does the timberwolf lighten the horizon with hope. When the rain let loose, the clouds homogenized. Charcoal and muddied is the world above the road, cars, and dark tree-lined hills.

It was the week after that truly led to the escalation of his hopes. Anastasia was finally called on the following Monday, three days from the movie and the hug and the wave goodbye. The talking was good and she sounded excited to hear from him. They conveyed their weekends to each other. Augustus fought to hold back telling her about the letter he had sent her. He is no good with surprises, but he caught swift his tongue with a mantra of discipline and the benefits of valuing things as they deserve. Anastasia would soon enough receive a poem about winter trees by Sylvia Plath. A poem bitter, crisp, and beautiful. A short simple note was attached to it signed with a single simple "A."

Anastasia loved trees, she knew the names of many. The poem was an old favorite of his and now, like many of his favorite things, it reminded him of her. Apparently he wanted it to remind her of him.

With the advent of summer, they could find no time to meet during that week. They talked again on Tuesday. Wednesday he waited for her to call. Augustus would not call, oh no. She must have received the letter at least by then. So he waited and he thought and he tried not to think. His world fell apart around him and he waited. As the sheltering bough of school slipped away in the summer's sudden wind and the hard light of loneliness and real-worldliness burned down, he waited. Any time he left his expired dormitory room to try to either replace his seasonal job or his seasonal home, he checked his voicemail half-hourly. Thursday Augustus broke down and called Anastasia.

Anastasia sounded enthusiastic about getting together; the weekend was bad for her. Augustus told her Monday he planned to take his best friend out for a surprise birthday dinner. Many others would be coming, but none that Anastasia knew. She had yet to meet birthday boy Sadius, though Augustus had talked much about him. Quickly and willingly, she agreed to attend. Regardless of the drive, she said she wanted to be there. He didn't think she'd want to come. She truly was exceptional to be enthused by a situation that would frighten the frailer, more common female peers Augustus was used to. They set a meeting time for Monday. Panicked and giddy with nerves of volcanic stomach acid, he bounced off of the phone to share the news with Sadius and really anyone who would listen.

The weekend went well on many fronts. A job came through, a good one. A home was found, up north and inexpensive. To Augustus these were not achievements, they were ends to distractions. His shoulders were lighter of major burdens, but still his middle raged sour and anxious. His jeans were there to dry his palms while his thoughts teemed with paranoiac worry and euphoric memory. He was a brew, stirred and seeking balance. She could even be this balance once the beginning was traversed. When not moving all of his books, cd's, and clothes to his new room, he planned Monday.

On Monday, it wasn't as if Augustus used Sadius and his birth as a way of seeing Anastasia. His manipulations were not that clumsy or simple. Monday was Sadius' day. This was known. It was known because Augustus said so. Augustus organized everything. Sadius was the man of honor and Augustus was the loving friend. In his labors for love and his merit of friendship, Augustus became the hero. He knew Sadius felt it. The night was an expressive play or dialectic of love between two friends, one giving and one receiving, interchangeably. Glowing, self-conscious, and proud, Augustus prayed that Anastasia noticed. He was selling himself, his lovability, and his ability to love through Sadius to her. He paid for everything; he lavished on the luxury. Every movement and happening he staged. Every door, he caught; every joke, he threw out. He was funny, considerate, and exciting. All the while he smiled at Anastasia, fit her into the conversation and tried to keep her happy. Augustus tried to make everything perfect.

In the car back to the dorms, to Augustus' barren room, Anastasia yawned like a cat. She said she was tired. If she was to drive home tonight, which she must, first she must rest. With all the best intentions from what he thought was all points of view, Augustus offered his room. After a hug of love, camaraderie, and dismissal, Augustus allowed the birthday boy to return to his respective room with the other celebratory guests and then led Anastasia to his, to rest. But, ah, in his room she immediately flopped on his bed, yes, his very bed. Her head was on his pillow, her hair spilling about his nocturnal sanctuary covering his dream-nest like so many of the past nights. Except this was real, she was real. She yawned, stretched, and contracted all her muscles with feline precision and then relaxed them all into a fetal curl with a smile like a little girl, like a princess in a world of her making; all of which was on his bed, the only lingering personalized part of this soon to be abandoned shelter.

Augustus watched. Watching and pretending not to watch, surveying his room, pretending to busy with tidying, sitting down into reading, pretending to read, pretending that every little one of her movements was not somehow tied directly into his joy, his sense of meaning, his heart's bleeding explanation for beating. He was glad to need her. Needing her was what he needed. He was so excited to feel as if he was on the threshold of an ending and a new beginning. Was this a doorway into one's self through another? Was this…? It was growing harder for Augustus to hold strong the dyke of sap that had built and flooded in him since the first meeting with Anastasia. The social confidence he still felt from hosting a winning birthday for Sadius was reaching the border of control. He was checking himself less. He was getting high on her closeness, and not just a little bit foolhardy. Guards were dropping. His mind read its own signs. Anything was a symbol and optimism was harder to question. After all, Augustus had been waiting for quite some time for it to be okay to be happy. And here she lay in his bed, resting, smiling, needing him.

And then she spoke. At first she only sat up and asked for a cigarette. He lit her one and ventured one for himself. But then she really spoke. Anastasia had a way of starting sentences with "Oh," either excited and exclamatory or sympathetic, and sometimes even seemingly vocative, that just made Augustus swoon and listen like a child in awe. Beginning with the "Oh," as if she startled herself out of her rest with her own enthusiasm, Anastasia spoke of a movie or maybe a song or a book she had read or a poem and how that work housed some connection that she must convey to Augustus. That must have lead to him talking. Again they agreed and once again and again. Soon they spoke of them, *them*. Dream plans for the future were made and many places needed to be traveled to and seen, either him showing her or her showing him or discovering together. They were glad to have found each other. She told him how close she felt to him and that she could tell him anything. He was ready for the confidence of her heart, he was ready for anything. She told him about her boyfriend, who is eleven years older than she, who she has been seeing for three years. She told him how she can't even tell her mother, who has always been a great confidant. For three years, her mother didn't even know, but now he knew.

Of course she couldn't tell anyone else at school, what would people think, how could she explain, as she told Augustus, the relationship was so abstract.

Augustus had reached a point of great intimacy with Anastasia that night. After he quieted his seismic heart, and disguised his face with conversational questions and strained happiness for her, he was even able to relax into talking about his past relationships. When it had gotten late and they had talked a lot, he walked her to her car. The goodbye hug felt different and then he let her leave. He shuddered to walk back to his room alone. He was cold and he wanted to cry. He felt betrayed, but he knew he couldn't blame her. He hated that he could not blame her. How could he be so wrong? How could she not feel the same way?

Augustus still asks himself these questions in the rain. He is at peace driving, numbed by nicotine and dense air. There is a summer coolness in his condensation cocoon. He hasn't been able to call her since that Monday night. That was four days ago and he has kept himself busy with moving. In case she called, though he hoped she wouldn't, he had moving as an excuse. He just didn't know what to say. Could he really just ask her why she doesn't love him? Maybe she does, but not the way he wants. And so he is selfish, stubborn, and silent. His rage is vanity so he bites it tight. On the highway, his car is a silver segment of a wet metal millipede, stamping slow and drudgely on the flattened terra. He is locked in with others, commuters, homeward bound, waiting his turn. Through his windows he can see no farther than his dark charcoal dome will allow. Every sigh is smoke and it's as if he makes his own clouds.

Further up the road, not many miles, I have passed the storm. From the car, road-wind carries rain-beads away, back behind me, quick with the speed I propel us forward. Angling rays of gold heat and hope, the prodigal sun, cut through thin fluff strips of cloud scraping the sky's height. Across the horizon scuttle and skid airy sun-blanched dustball clouds, losing mass with momentum, losing substance with sunlight. I still drive north and the mountains and their trees of many greens seem to exhale, tired and brave, after a passionate storm more filling than draining. It was a storm that whet and met a thirst, costing little than a lesson in courage and security. The trees of many greens held tight to a soil as temporal and shifting as any other part of nature. Still the mountains look the same and strong, they have weathered well; they have done this before. And they will do it again. Farther up the road, in the direction I barrel, the sun beats free and wild. On the forward horizon, the northern horizon, the road and trees are long dry. Augustus should see what I see in that distant, approaching vanishing point. He should know that the last cottonball tumbleweed cloud blew west across the sky's plain already. I roll the window down and the warm air slides in, fresh, and I exhale among the many trees as the sun tingles tall the hair on my left arm. Augustus should know this. I wish I could tell him.

OUROBOROS

SHE WAS SO COMFORTABLE giving herself over to what he was doing that her ass rested with almost all of her weight on his throat and her thighs closed tightly around his face. He thought this could be a sweet place to die, in her thighs. The action for him was as pleasurable as the place. He licked swiftly, not franticly, and controlled against her clitoris as the rest of her weight went into the headboard through her gripping hands. He did not want to stop or rest until she was done, so he breathed in and out through his nose. Out went his breath and in went her taste and smell. He enjoyed it, he always did; he loved her. Thinking of his placement, her sounds, her smell, and her body was enough to make him come hands-free, so he tried to take his mind away as he worked...

✳

YOU, READER, might think his mind went to other women in free sensory association, but sexually he was always present with her. She was not the first, but in his mind and heart she was the only and, he hoped, last. The thought of her being the last tied in with the morbid sexual humor of his potential demise from her ass's pressure on his throat. Beyond that, the tangy sweet musk of her secretions brought him to memories of kissing her neck publicly, maybe while shopping or standing behind her at a concert. Transposing his situation presently to the other times and actions his memory created just fueled his arousal, and own imminent bodily release, and he had to back off those thoughts. The memories created anew into fantasies of slipping into a dressing room of an apparel store or a venue bathroom were too delicious. Instead he tried to veer his thoughts further away from this time and context while his tongue and lips ardently operated in this connection of love, work, operation, and offering. But the connection was the key for him, the connection itself was room for mental play at theorizing and philosophizing. An image they mutually loved began to represent for him their mutual love. OUROBOROS (ôr-rŏb'-ôr-rŭs). But he could not dwell on its obvious sexual implications, you see, in his situation, he had to take it elsewhere…For a flash, as he thought of how he was holding her up with his face and neck, he thought of Atlas and his myth…And through that up crept an eschatological veer from the traditional cyclicality of…

OUROBOROS. He could die here, he had already thought, a sweet death, we remember his postulating, so that again might be influencing the new finality he is finding in OUROBOROS. He knew the literal meaning of OUROBOROS, *tail-eater*, but it was too sexual to think of. As he thought for a moment of twisting the eschatology, a line of Eliot's own eschatological twisting crept up into his thoughts, "Not with a bang but a whimper." Was it a literary association or was it a bang of her hands on the headboard, a whimper of her lips/while he made tremble her hips? That is he, our hero, distracting himself through rhyme, following the sounds of words away from their meaning, but this showed he was on a good track towards mental stability and focus…

He returned towards OUROBOROS, seeing it like a cartoon character reborn from myth, like Marvel's Thor. The snake takes its tail in its mouth. That is the image. The story of the symbol connotes Heraclitus, Paracelsus, alchemy, Nietzsche, and... Eternal Return...Still it is a snake whose eyes are too big for its stomach...Tail is too big for its appetite...Eyes are too big for its tail...He tried them all with pleasure in the quest for the *bon mot*. We are trained to see it as a never ending cycle of devouring, he pondered, but what if it does not eat, rinse, and repeat. What if he cannot eat himself? There is solipsism here, Narcissism (image and myth are flashed), even Onanism (another flash of myth, but with image avoided). The poor snake desires only itself, desires to the point of consumption: unity.

You are what you eat and It wants to eat Itself until It becomes Itself; maybe becomes Itself totally; *hoc est corpus meum en toto*; *ad nauseum*...

Can one eat one's own mass?

What is then consumed, what is consuming?

He presented these big questions before his disembodied mind—now far from, though for the sake of, the rhythmically flickering tongue and sucking lips—but chooses not to follow them too far into pointless terrain. The image itself gave enough fodder for basic thought and concise decision making. The snake would choke. The positioning of the snake in the image is even hazardous in appearance. For the snake to get the tail to any depth in its mouth, it would be difficult to get it out.

Eternal Return is a misinterpretation. Ouroboros is the tail choker, gagging on itself. Loving oneself to the point of binging, trapped in that point, the position of consumption, and unable to purge. This is the way the world will end, not with a bang, or whimper, but a gurgle, choking on oneself. Our desires, loves, threaten to consume us in our consumption. His mind went wild with environmental and capitalistic analogies. He thought he had solved the problems of the world, unlocked the keys to our fate, and maybe now, our not so inevitable destruction. He was overjoyed and bit down—rather gummed down—with his lips, to her lips, pressurizing and sweetly pulverizing with his tongue on her clitoris as she tightened the grip of her hands on the headboard, her thighs on his cheeks, her ass-cheeks on his throat and she came—floodingly, loudly, thunderously. His mind went heavy, then light, then blank, coming with her… hands-free…into…OBLIVION.

STAN OF CHANGES

AFTER THIRTY-EIGHT YEARS, the universe revealed to Stan his destiny through a typo in an intra-office memo. With the recent downturn of the economy, the company was going through a period of readjustment. Stan's position as the Head of Administrative Acquisitions and Maintenance Coordination, though by no means glamorous, was relatively secure. No matter how many people worked in the office, they would always need such office supplies as printer paper, pens, white out, computers, chairs, and desks and the executives could not be expected to make purchases themselves. There was also the constant need for IT tech support, printer repair, and maintenance of the heating and air conditioning systems for the building that warranted full-time attention. No, Stan wasn't going anywhere, unless the whole office was closed and downsized. This basic fact did not stop Stan from worrying.

It was the new consultant, Ms. Sweetin, brought in to streamline the operations and increase efficiency, who really worried him. She worried everyone in the office, and her confident and perky demeanor gave off the impression of a secret ruthlessness that truly struck fear into employee hearts, especially the heart of Stan. When she entered the office in the morning, the resonance of her heels on the tile of the entranceway sounded distinct from anyone else's, driving Stan's pulse into a harder rhythm than it was previously pounding in expectation of her entrance. Once her heels left the tiles and hit the carpet that covered the whole office except for the conference room, their silence—or stealth mode—became a more dangerous trigger to Stan's anxiety, his right hand trembling uncontrollably on his coffee mug. He would perk his ears to listen to her high, lilting voice as it cheerfully greeted every person she passed, from cubicle to cubicle, on the way to her office, mapping her direction and progress away from him. After he knew she was contained, he would reflexively dab a Kleenex to the sweat on his bald head and adjust the belt across his rotund gut repeatedly until he could resume work.

For the first week, his terror was Pavlovian, waiting for her to enter, hearing her enter and go stealth, listening for her to make her way to her office, and then waiting for the axe. That first week saw little else of Ms. Sweetin, as she spent most of the time in her office or the conference room, going over the employment records, office productivity reports, past quarter budgets and earnings, and meeting regularly with the CFO. Stan went about his day noticeably shaken and disturbed to any who cared to notice, but most people around the office didn't normally notice Stan. When there was a paper jam or computer problem or some supply ran low, the executives normally just told the receptionist, Kara. She then called, texted, or walked a post-it note over to Stan with the request or problem.

Attractive, blond, and practically translucent, Kara was a receptionist and nothing more. She was hired for that position, assumed that title, and gave no thought to any other function other than reception. She smiled when people entered the office, receiving them. She smiled when she answered the phone, receiving the call. As far as Kara was concerned, anything else was Stan's job. When Kara was fired at 4:30 on the Friday at the end of Ms. Sweetin's first week, Stan began to truly panic, believing that he was next.

That weekend was a rough one for Stan. His one bedroom apartment, full of all his favorite Marvel and DC comic super heroes and Simpsons characters lining the walls—some hermetically sealed, some out and ready for action—was less welcoming and inspirational than normal. As quick as any other weekend, he was out of his sweaty work clothes and in his purple bathrobe with random stars taped to the back, but he couldn't relax. He ate a whole low-fat Hungry Man Family Size chicken pot pie, his favorite, to no avail. Stan was plagued by foreboding. After a TiVo'ed episode of "Battlestar Galactica," he courted sleep forcefully with the aid of allergy medicine.

Saturday was no different. No different as far as his normal activities and no different as far as his mounting anxiety level. He woke late and set about his work. It began with cereal, then television, then the full round-up of his favorite internet sites, and then back into his star charts. The coverage of the window shades was tightened and the lights were turned out. The star charts glowed in the dark on the breakfast table, the only table, and the stars covering half the ceiling glowed too. He was ready to put up Orion, the hunter, the greatest superhero in the night sky. All the pieces fit, leading to this great figure, squared off and strong. Stan knew nothing more about the constellation Orion than the name and the description of "hunter," yet making that shape on his ceiling with plastic stars brought to life the image in a way that stirred his soul.

By night he would be tired of, and from, this activity and with the shades still drawn to the true night sky he would turn in early, as he often did on weekends. Sunday was more of the same for his project, filling in plastic stars to accentuate the superhero in the sky, but with every increasing breath, before he finally forced his way to sleep, his heart felt like it might explode.

Monday was the fated day for Stan, the day of destiny, he felt it in his bones, and the ache of his stomach, and he supposed it was a destiny of doom, but Stan was often wrong about what the universe had in store for him. His coffee mug was not joking when it declared that he hated Mondays, and this felt like the worst he had ever woken up to. He arrived before everyone else and passed Kara's empty desk on the way to his own. Her desk was always empty when he arrived, everyone's was, but he knew hers would remain empty and he read this as an omen. He sat and waited, waited for each hand on the door, each heel to the tiles, until eventually the sound of her heels, different from every other sound of footwear to the very same tiles.

She was the fifth person to arrive, Ms. Sweetin, and once she hit stealth mode she was straight on down the *good morning* line to her office. Stan could barely gasp. He could barely sip enough coffee to wet his dry mouth and throat. *It is coming*, he thought, *it is coming*, over and over again. Until it came, after an hour, on his desk, dropped off by Ms. Sweetin herself with a smile and wink: an intra-office memo. It began with introductions, re-introductions actually, the usual, *As you all my know, I am Ms. Janet Sweetin, and I am here to better your work environment through an increase in productivity through greater efficiency...*

Stan continued to read down through all of the talk about *restructuring,* and *cultivating resources through valuing what is working* and *eliminating what isn't,* waiting for that axe, and feeling the hairs at the back of his neck stand in expectation of the blade. His peripheral vision caught the best of him, and he picked up a trace of his name further down the page than he had yet to read. He rushed to that paragraph. Reading fast, his comprehension was one step behind the words, *As you all have noticed, the receptionist, Kara, was let go on Friday and in lieu of replacing her we are reallocating all of her duties to where they belonged in the first place. Stan, The Head of Administrative Acquisitions and Maintenance Coordination, will be taking on the surplus duties and responsibilities. All functions of an Office*

Manager will be his. Please continue to operate as you always have and stay the course, but if anything should arise, please notify Stan of Changes. He can make it happen!

He read it again. And again. Slower and slower, drawing his mind, and his lips, over each word, mouthing them out. It was that last sentence that initially got him; it ended with an exclamation point. But before it, the three sentences before it, all needed review. Kara was gone. She would not be replaced. He was mentioned with his title. Then a new title, *Office Manager*, all the functions of which will be his. That, he was slowly digesting. But the second to last sentence, it came on so cavalierly, addressing everyone about upholding protocol, and yet did it not end with another title? Did he have that right? He was Stan, Head of Administrative Acquisitions and Maintenance Coordinator, who assumed all the functions of an Office Manager, and was now dubbed *Stan of Changes*? That is what it said, in caps: *Stan of Changes. He can make it happen!*

That night he went home to a welcome of painted plastic fanfare lining the walls. He turned on the television, but forgot it was on while he heated his dinner. He didn't put his purple bathrobe on, but nonetheless stripped down and drew it from the closet. At the kitchen table, Stan laid the bathrobe down and collected some plastic stars, seven large and two small. Removing the taped stars from the purple cloth and plugging in his hot glue gun to warm up, he brought his dinner from the microwave to the counter by the table.

Seven stars he glued in place, each one just right, with the two smaller ones for the tip of the sword and top of the head. Dutifully, he waited for them to dry before he put on the robe. He didn't even finish his Hungry Man. He opened the window shades, and as he stood up against the night, with the sky and stars all around him, the constellation shape he bore fit in perfectly.

ALL THINGS RESOUND

A GHOST STORY

*Actions have resonance. Actions are things. All things resound.
They continue to resound in the place they happened.*

DRIVING BACK HOME one night from visiting her mother in Atlanta, last Tuesday actually, Lara sung along with the stereo, the low highway rolling by with yellow ticks of paint and reflectors in the dark. The song was melancholy with a refrain to belt out legato and intense, allowing Lara to emote while belting, tears forced from her eyes. The last time she heard this song was through headphones in the much more public location of the treadmill at the gym. She couldn't do her listen then the justice that she could now. As it ended, she stopped at one of the annoying stoplights on this highway.

She started back off from the light into the darkness, building up speed again, and she saw a flicker of light ahead on the right shoulder. She wondered what it was. It was a quick intense wonder and she released the gas gradually to look. When she saw it was a candle flickering at a flower-decked cross, she braked and pulled over.

The night was chilly, but she left the car without getting her jacket from the back seat. She hit the hazards and shut the door, scanning the night. Whoever lit the candle was gone, for how long she didn't know, but it was still lit against the windy whizz of the cars on the highway. Lara knew what the cross meant, and she always thought the concept was strange. Why come here when the person is most likely buried somewhere else? Do the loved ones, family members, always go to both, here and the grave? She thought they probably went to the latter on the birthdays and here on the other day.

Today must be that day, she thought, and this must be the spot. Lara stood in front of the cross. Three cars passed behind her, all big sport utility vehicles, all fifteen miles per hour over the speed limit and the wind they brought cut through the knit tights she wore under her skirt. The flame flickered, flickered, flickered, cutting hard back against the wind each time in its partial glass enclosure, finally standing hard again.

This was the spot.

Lara turned around and looked at the highway. It didn't look so violent now. There were cars with their lights far back to the left, behind the red light, and far taillights to the right horizon, but right here, right now, it was a dark peaceful place. She lowered at the knees and sat down her dark skirt into the cool damp earth.

Her ass cooled and a chill went up her back. She lay her legs out flat and slowly down her back went to the earth; just a t-shirt marring little of its chill. The flickers of the candle were just above her head. Every few flicks brought the shape of the cross or the flowers, or both, a terrifying shadow. Lara held her breath with such force she choked. She coughed and jerked against the earth, loosening it and generating more chills. It was hard to breathe, hard to catch her breath again. The white lights on the horizon to the left closed in on her. She held tight to her breath, pressed her back to the slight hill of the ground, and the candle went out as the torrent of traffic overtook where she was.

In that one moment, in that place, there was so much noise from the cars, released from the traffic light, Lara could hear nothing; from the bright of their lights she could see nothing; from the intense pain of the place she could feel nothing, and through the thudding off-time beat of death her heart could not complete. When the traffic abated and the she could see again and hear again her breath released and her heartbeat resumed.

Lara knew everything and felt it all, all the pain. She rolled to her side to retch, and retching and rolling slushed in the wide puddle she had released and in which she now lay. It was awful, all awful. She stood and whipped her face with her hand and against her short sleeve. She was achy and cold, wet from the waist most of the way down. Without turning to look back at the cross, flowers, or candle—the cross made and laid by Jose's mother Marisol, and the flowers from both his Tia Julieta and Tio Juan, and the candle placed and lit tonight by his sister Miryam—she slowly staggered down the hill to her car.

Pushing her legs through the ache she got to the car swiftly. On the hillside of the car she leaned on the back passenger for a moment to catch herself. She needed to get out of here fast. She got in the car and gunned it, just drove, off from the shoulder and out down the highway, as a panic over took her and her nerve endings. She cried and wanted to scream and punch the wheel, but held it, she had to focus and get away. Twenty miles and fifteen minutes down the road she pulled over on the shoulder and got out to run around to the side and retched again. Ducking down into the back seat she took off her t-shirt and wiped her face with it, cleaning her mouth and dabbing at her eyes. Luckily the jacket she had with her was a raincoat-style and came down to her mid-thigh. She removed her skirt, tights, and panties all in one motion, stepping out of her boots to get it all down. With a clean corner of the t-shirt she wiped at herself where she was still wet and then balled all her clothes up into a wet gross mess and shoved it into a plastic grocery bag littering the floor of her car. Lara then stood with the jacket on and put her back to the road to button it. With a newspaper from the backseat she padded the driver's seat so she wouldn't get filthy again and got in to leave.

*

WHY ME, was all Lara thought the rest of the way back to Athens. It had all already happened to Jose, why did she need to feel it all too. It lingered in her memory, her whole body, her muscle memory, in a way that it couldn't for Jose, for he was dead. She kept wanting to scream but instead just ached and drove. Other than "why me," she did think "poor Jose," but what he felt only lasted a moment whereas for her it continued to linger; she could even see the car the hit him, hear the crunch of plastic bumpers and metal frames, and feel again and again the metal into skin and into bone. Her seatbelt felt so tight as she drove, Lara felt the way it choked the breath out of Jose, but she was scared to take it off.

She needed to go straight to the library. Lara had been cutting close the drive all night. She left Atlanta with just enough time. The stop at the flickering candle slowed her down and now she had no time to remedy the situation that she was naked under her coat except for a bra. She could call in, but what would she say, "I see dead people, or really just one dead guy, but mostly I just feel him, the pain of his death;" and the absurd humor in this potential interchange gave some levity to her state. But Lara still couldn't think straight and come with any good excuse, passively with no better option to cross her mind she headed to the library for her late evening shift.

80

When she pulled into the parking deck a clear thought cut through the residual ache and lit upon her consciousness, *Rose*. Rose would be working the front desk. Rose is always either to or from the gym on one end of her shift or the other. Rose would have a change of clothes, gym clothes at least.

Lara grabbed her purse and phone and ran from the deck into the library. Rose greeted her with a smile at the front desk.

"Hey girl, why you rushing, you are just in time, and just in time to do a lot of nothing."

"Hi Rose," she gasped out of breath, "do you have your gym bag with you, or is it in your car? Please say you have it."

"I have it, Jeez, I was gonna go late after work. Why?"

"Excellent," Lara leaned on the desk and then paced in a circle catching more breath. "Can I borrow your gym clothes right now? Maybe you will have time to go by the dorm before the gym after work for more. Please, its important."

"You need my gym clothes? Why? What are you wearing under that coat? Girl, what have you been up to? Seriously?"

"Please, I can't really explain. Will you just help me out?"

"Sure, relax, its fine, here you go," and Rose reached down beneath the high desk and drew up a red and black gym bag. "But you owe me a story at least and an explanation of why I wasn't invited to whatever craziness you have been up to."

Lara took the bag and agreed, laughing off her friend. She clocked in and then changed in the bathroom glad that she and Rose were roughly the same size, except for in the chest, but luckily her bra had survived the filth and soiling. She quickly cleaned her face and crotch the best she could with hand soap and set to work. There was a full cart of books needing to be reshelved and she hoped the methodical mindless repetition of her slow uneventful job would cool and calm her down.

What was on the cart brought her first to the third floor and then up to the sixth. Up and down the stacks she breathed slowly, focusing on each breath, like she learned in yoga. She paid close attention to call numbers and her work and her mind wandered about the books, up and down each aisle, film theory, biographies of directors, then African oral literature and folk traditions. It seemed funny to her that all of this should be on the same floor, but there were only seven floors so it had to all mix together in some way. At the end of an aisle Lara noticed a wooden chair off in the corner, a chair that should be at one of the study tables in the floor's common area near the elevators. This section of the sixth floor was the most private part of the library, and Lara knew, though not first hand, of its reputation as a popular make-out spot. Most likely explains the chair, either way, it was her job to straighten up behind the library visitors so she went to get it.

The chair faced the plain off-white corner, cold and isolated and for the second time tonight Lara felt a compulsion, she needed to sit in the chair. The second she sat down she shut her eyes and felt the tongue. She opened her eyes and there was no one around but her eyes slammed shut again and she felt the tongue again. It was right against her, it was right against her and it was *right*. A boy's face flashed before her shut eyes, a boy she had never seen before, his eyes shut too, just going to town and humming and she could feel the humming burn-cooly out from the spot into her thighs; and then a different boy's face, and then a girl's. Lara pulled her eyes, open no one around. There was a girl's face she didn't know, a second ago before her shut eyes, between her legs, but they weren't her legs, and the girl was more than just tongue, she was lips and mouth and sucking, so warm. And then Lara felt the waves, three hard breaking waves over her, stiffening everything, boiling her blood. The first two were familiar, similar to long orgasm waves she had felt before but the last broke shorter, cresting earlier, in three stalls and jerks and then nothing, no resolution. Her hair follicles on her head and down her arms, toes, and fingertips tingled as she drooped out of the chair and crawled into the stacks towards her cart.

All the pain from earlier was gone, and the aches had transformed; Lara was spent. Slowly she pulled herself up to sort of slump against the cart. She hadn't bothered to borrow panties from Rose's bag, but now the gray sweat pants she did borrow were a wet shade darker in the worst, most obvious location. Lara was done. She was done with this night. She was spent, wet, and freaked out. She was so done with other people's feelings, other people's experiences. She didn't feel like herself and she didn't feel real.

Lara rolled the cart as cover in front of her to the elevator and down to her coat for better cover. She clocked out and on her way past the front desk she told Rose to tell their supervisor she was sick, it was food poisoning, she had to go. Lara was very done with this night.

Over the next few years these moments of heightened sensitivity continued to occur, but never as bad as this first night, never two in one day. The world became a minefield for Lara, and as she slowly understood what was happening, she became increasingly careful of where she sat or lay down, where she let herself relax with her guard down. She could never really know though, hence the minefield feeling. She never told anyone about these experiences and could think of no practical use for this ability of hers. Her "sensitivity to locations" was more a curse than a power. Mostly it was just disruptive and embarrassing, but she did learn to control her reactions to some degree. Sadly, all her practice and preparation couldn't prepare her for that one fateful night where and when she learned how her father really died and what kind of person her mother really was.

THE WORM

The Worm turns…It is expected…

See the Worm…It arrives like it has never been gone…

The Worm…See the Worm…See it arise and see it turn, the Conquering Worm…It is here…It sees by knowing, seeing without eyes…No eyes, but a mouth at both ends…And an anus at both ends…The same both ends…For the Worm may not begin, but the Worm never ends…It is here for you, for us, for me…To eat, then shit…To eat, then vomit…It is all the same with the Worm…All without turning…

And still the Worm turns…It turns and it rears…Its body is thick rings of muscle…It is just a long lower torso on all sides… Thick rings like abdominal muscles…Covered in sharp wire hairs like…nails…sharp nails…How it sees, how it feels, how it knows… With each turn and ripple the nail-hairs dig and trigger…They are antennae…They are divining rods…Here it comes now…The Worm is turning…

✳

PETER CLOSED THE NOTEBOOK. He tried to write the Worm away but still it followed. Notebook shut. Eyes open. Still the worm. Sometimes it worked. This was not one of those times. The Worm went beyond the page. The Worm was a page-eater.

Something sightless. Something with no discernment between eating, vomiting, or shitting. A rolling mass of muscles sharp to the touch and, with every move, sightlessly knowing. It was the perfect horror for Peter.

There is no way the other students in Study Hall could feel like he felt. They read or wrote silently in their notebooks, being normal students doing homework. Now as he rubbed his eyes, tried to rub the Worm from his eyes, and looked around he felt so alone. But Peter was never alone, he had the Worm.

✳

PETER'S MOTHER meant well. She meant well all seventeen years of his life. She meant well when she wasn't around because it meant that she was working hard to support her child and self. She meant well when she was around, even when she was telling Peter what to do, because it meant she cared enough to take an interest in his life. And she especially meant well when he was a small child and she read great literature to him every night in bed. It so happened that one of the books of classic literature she read to Peter was a collection by Edgar Allan Poe. This book was among the likes of Edith Hamilton's *Mythology* and *Aesop's Fables* and assorted fairy tales. What she loved about the Poe was that his poems rhymed and flowed so well; she found them perfect for a child. Sometimes she would move on to the short stories. Some had poems in them. Ligeia was like this. The subject matter was pretty dark, but the ages at which she read it to him she assumed he didn't understand, maybe he just enjoyed the rhythms and rhymes from the poem it contained, its name was "The Conqueror Worm." She only read him Ligeia three times between the ages of two to five. That was all it took.

✳

It GREW from the pages of Poe, grew and changed with Peter over the years. As if it expanded with his consciousness, it constantly bent and realigned its grasp upon him. The Worm became the dark part of him, where all fears and anxieties went. But that is just the psychology. To compare the Worm to the imaginary friends of other children would not be fair to Peter.

For Peter, the Worm was very real in its presence and potentiality. When he slept the Worm was there behind every image. He could see a friend, his mother, Superman, and the Worm would turn and that would be the new dream. No more friend, no more mother, no more Superman, just the Worm, turning and eating and vomiting and shitting, all at once, every end, every movement.

Daydreaming was no different. Each thought needed no more than three steps to connect back to the Worm.

✳

BY AGE TEN he saw the Worm everywhere, in every blink, either end of the blink, open or closed. School was tough, but nothing was really easy. He saw the Worm in his teachers' eyes, turning around in the irises and threading through the pupils. He tried to sing it away. He fought his fears with art from an early age. It was not consciously calculated, only a reflex, deep in his humanity. No one had ever told him that "Ring Around the Rosie" fought the plague. Not as didactic, his song, nevertheless at ten he began to sing:

Fingers or toes
Or even a long nose
Anything can be
The Worm

Fingers or toes
Or even a long nose
Anything can be
The Worm

Over and over to a crazy but soothing rhythm like:

Bum ba da da
Bum ba da da da
Bum ba da da…
Da Da!

But that is what it was like. The Worm was everywhere and to the rhythm of:

Bum ba da da
Bum ba da da da
Bum ba da da…
Da Da!

He sang and sang under his breath and when he was lucky the rhythm took the Worm away from every finger or toe or even long nose.

※

Now, AT SEVENTEEN, as he tried to write it away, he went through many notebooks. The Worm was a page-eater and ate oh, so many pages. Peter wrote everywhere, all the time. It seemed to be his only control, his only power, no matter how ineffectual, against the Worm. When he was younger, scratch paper would do, but as this attempt gained seriousness, he needed better equipment. He thought the school bag and the constant homework given a high school student were good cover for the ever-present notebooks. Cheap was okay, but the more plentiful the pages the better.

Peter's mother bought *Writer's Market* books for her son and any literary magazine she saw that contained short stories. She left them all over the house. One day he would be a great writer, she believed. She was so proud of how hard he worked, writing all the time. And she applauded herself for all the great literature she read to him when he was a child. She had no idea what she really put inside him.

Peter was the love of her life, her raison d'être, and his success would be her success. This writing must come to something, he worked so hard all the time. He must be a budding novelist, she thought, to fill so many notebooks. She fought so hard peeking into just one, just one of those marble composition books stacked all over his bedroom. Soon he would graduate and every college she suggested had a good English Literature program with Creative Writing. He had such a solid foundation already— the love of literature she provided from a very early age and all this writing practice he has been doing.

✳

THIS FINAL SEMESTER of his senior year, Peter had a pretty easy schedule. After Study Hall, his seventh and final period was Gym. This was the highlight of the day. He could run a little track and then load up his backpack and run home from school still in his gym clothes. Running was good; there were moments when his mind cleared and there was nothing, not even the Worm. And then the endorphins came and there was a slight high and another moment of Worm respite.

Today—after Study Hall, then Gym—followed that same pattern of the semester. Peter ran home with his backpack on.

As it was Friday, his mother would be home from work early and they could maybe go shopping together before dinner. Since it would be summer soon, and then college, he actually wanted to spend as much time as possible with his mother, when she wasn't nagging him.

Peter walked into the house and called out a general greeting to his mother, wherever she was, as he headed towards his bedroom. When he opened the door he found her there, sitting on his bed. Every surface of his room—floor, desk, dresser, and bed—was covered with open notebooks. His mother had one on her lap and staring down at it, she was crying and blinking rapidly.

Oh, what joy and elation Peter now felt. Maybe he was no longer alone with the Worm? Maybe it could even go back to from whence it came? Maybe the Worm won't win?

THREE SISTERS
FROM OHIO

HE COULD REMEMBER how he met them, but he couldn't understand how he had gotten in so very deep. It is all a furious blur between the first introduction and finding himself here. One day he was at a bullfight in Valencia with a Canadian couple he had met in Barcelona. He was downing beers and snapping photos for the American Magazine that paid his bills. Hiding behind his long-distance lens and protecting his Cruz Campo from the splashes of dust and sand, he saw his first bull, like a bloody flower, wilt to the ground in darkness as a cloud covered the six o'clock sun. The Canadian woman, Janine, shattered her silent awe with a torrent of tears and ran from the stands. But he could not be disturbed, even when her boyfriend Stanish said, "I guess I should check on her, ay, watch my beer," and left his side. He watched as the three horses came out, with the harness behind them, and the bull was hooked on. He watched the turns they took around the ring, boastfully, while the dust cast upward by the dragged cadaver. The Nikon shutter snapped rapid snaps and our hero wondered whether a piece of himself was being pulled out of the ring with the bull, to be burned in some Spanish back alley pyre. Pictures of Picasso's virile raping Minotaur came to mind, along with thoughts that maybe this tradition was some revenge for what happened to Europa and Io, and he smirked sadly at the notion of fitting that into his story. He couldn't watch anymore. Up the stairs, he made no eye contact. Spanish faces showed their anxiety and rapture as another bull charged the ring behind his back.

In the lobby, his drunken gaze directed his stagger towards the Canadians. Janine's tears had found friends. She and Stanish were not alone. "That was some sick shit, ay? Janine met these American girls who couldn't handle it either." It was then that he was introduced to Bess, Becca, and Rita.

At first glance they annoyed him, and he found nothing attractive. He scolded his lack of journalistic objectivity, but allowed his world-weary caution to give his subjectivity some credence. They were all tall, one was fat, two were thin and gangly, and their handshake greetings were limp, moist, awkward things. His assessment of aesthetics was deeper than skin, and the ugliness he perceived went to the roots of their beings. His repulsion was enhanced with the sound of their voices. Similar, since they were sisters, their mid-western drawls all whined-out lazily and misted lethargic bitter venom. Siren songs for *norteamericanos* abroad. Internally, he struggled with mounting anxiety while listening to the story of their Ohio home. He was not lured. How were his ears blocked to the harpy wail affecting his comrades? His eyes tested the social waters and through the haze of beer and dead-bull-sorrow he could notice no suspicions from Janine and Stanish. For the sake of convenience, he followed the Canadian lead but could not readily accept the strangers.

How then, after all the polite traveler's etiquette, was a way found around all his misgivings and instincts to bring him here: strapped naked to a bed in some shitty room by the sea as the fat-oldest and the thin-youngest sisters hold his erect penis up and steady while the thin-middle sister, squatting naked over him, lowers down her black hole?

The fat one, in true bovine fashion, was named Bess and

they descended in age and size to Rita and then Becca. Oldest twenty-five, youngest nineteen. Rita was smack in the middle at twenty-two. It all starts to blur in a gradual fade upon leaving the bull stadium. The Canadians told the girls that they and the journalist had nowhere to sleep that night and planned to just squat in the station and wait for a morning train to Madrid. But the sisters, with their mid-western manners, would hear nothing of this. They had an apartment rented for a week, and this being their last night, saw no reason why guests could be a violation. The sisters even carried all of the bags and, not taking no for an answer, led the two Canadians and the journalist to their place in town.

Is that where he is now? He can smell the sea. It is so real, that smell. He fights the realness of it as he tries to hold back time, like holding back the lapping Mediterranean tide. He fights time as feebly as he fights the ever-descending hellhole poised above him on the underside of the squatting succubus. There is nothing he can do about the efforts of Bess and Becca, with their sweat-greased hands, to keep him hard and doomed. The three fates are eating him, nibble by nibble, with Rita awaiting the main course. He searches for how he got here, as knowing the way in can hopefully show the way back out.

He can summon some facts through the blurred images. He was in Europe on work while the Canadians were looking for a paradise of quaintness in which to rest and renew. But the sisters, they were on a different course. Their trip took the outward form of the American backpacker in Europe, riding the rails from capital to capital. A gift to all three from their father. A getaway and a consolation. Rita was stoking a grief, and what one sister felts the others matched and nurtured. Her husband died six months ago. The earth swallowed him up. It was an onsite construction accident. They drilled too deep and the earth split from an eye-like slit to a spreading moist smile to a gaping muddy maw with bristly sod-labia. In he went and down it took him. An open sewer with the rush of new air carried him to a watery death several blocks away. The crush of death was also a crush of defeat to all three sisters. Rita was the marrying one, and her Bill was chosen by all three. It was as if Bess and Becca had as much staked in the relationship and poor Bill never knew what he was getting himself into.

Rita was the homeliest with Ichabod Crane limbs and an upturned nose to hold her sagging glasses. Her dirty blonde hair frizzed just short of her shoulders. She strode a bit taller than Bess, with her long dark raven hair and rotund gut, though weight-worn posture was possibly responsible. Becca was petite at five foot ten and her dyed red hair labeled her as the rebellious youth. Her age also kept her in the graces of her sisters' ardent attention, who nurtured her eternal chastity. Bess, always like a mother to them all after their real mother passed away in childbirth with Becca, needed no more children or the distraction of men and was quick to sigh of her great age and responsibility. So it was all upon Rita, poor Rita, the bearer of their communal yearning, the middle one, outstanding in no way, whose duty it was to be the vessel for their enduring life and union with humanity.

As the three fates, the one eye they share is black and sweaty and drips down in a blank stare at his poor genitals. In that shadow, his manhood tries to retreat, but it is flanked on all sides by moisture and strokes and grips of steel. How did it get this far? Where are the Canadians, and how did they leave him to this? Will Stanish break in the door with a kick or a shoulder in the knick of time? The sins of the world, like so much road dirt, are cleansed from him with sweat as he struggles to live and fights to not despair. In this baptism by fire, the acid from Rita's cunt burns like no other pain, but can he burn to salvation just short of disintegration?

Rita's cunt makes contact and there is the sensation of being raked through a narrow rocky cavern as he barely breaks the surface. Giggles shrill, among steam and gray thick ash and hot bursting rag-water bubbles, rise up around him as Rita arches her back and cocks her head up like a wolf. Her oblong bubs wag loose and slushy. Her hands, for balance on his stomach, tighten and dig the nails under the surface of his skin. The laughter and wails of Bess and Becca bang loud against the walls, the murky air thickens more and the room is set a'pitch; they are witches at their stew and he is providing the stock. Rita howls and plunges her tight inferno deep down and his whole world goes black with pain, sounds of ripping and suffocating shrieks of vile glee.

...He feels a wave and yes he can still hear the ocean...faint but growing in his perception, the ocean...the journalist opens his eyes and it is just in time to see the wave arch above him, it is like a wall of liquid pearl glinting and reflecting, opaque, with blood-red jets bursting through it and then moving as one force with the wave and they blend into a sort of orange combination as mayonnaise and catsup make thousand island dressing, and the wave breaks over him, a sticky burst, a salty wash...from the muck he watches himself rise up...it is him, but only smaller, much smaller, bald and naked with webbed hands and feet dripping the orange goo, and before his eyes the webs dissolve and the goo drains down through the ground beneath his feet into the earth's tight ,warm sliver and he feels sad for the small naked him alone, so he reaches out to touch him and BAM his wrist is bound and shackled, he is pulled and dragged...through a cloud of dust, he can see it is a harness of three horses dragging him and he looks back at the little bald naked him who cries softly...through the distance he can see that the other him is no longer alone...yes, it is faint, but through the filter of haze and distance he sees three woman-shapes cloaked in black...they are kneeling down to the little him and wiping away his tears and then they lift him up and bear him like a king, and still from the distance he can see that they all four are waving goodbye… bells ring out on the bridles of the horses as he is paraded and dragged out of the bullring…triumphant applause…the fall of one bloody flower, one bloody rose…bells ring out…

✳

THE JOURNALIST wakes up with a kick and a gallop. He is in a bed, alone. The walls are gray and the floors are brown. A white sheet is on the floor to his right in a tousled pile and the bottom sheet dangles to his left, sweeping the floor. He looks down to how pale his body is and sweat drips from his forehead and back. His nakedness is all moist and his groin has a sweaty, cummy crusted reek. He rises weakly and finds his jeans on a chair and he pulls them on with a t-shirt. He finds one door to the rectangular room, makes his way, and opens it. New light rushes zealous, with new life, into the tomb and with it the smell of the sea. Down the stairs, he plods with a nauseated grog into the increasing sunlight. As if a symphony of light, it builds to a crescendo at the bottom of the stairs. The finale is an open-air lobby and café. The tables are empty, save one with Janine and Stanish having coffee and tostadas. They turn to greet the dazed traveling journalist. He squints through the rays of the morning sun.

"Look, just look, we told you Cadiz was beautiful, just look at that morning," and she was right and he nods to agree that the sparkling waves gently rolling up the beach, mere meters away from the porch cafe, are beautiful.

"Oh honey, he doesn't look so good, ay? Sit down, man, are you feeling okay? Honey, he doesn't look good"

"Of course not, with that fever last night, it's lucky he's alive," she says to Stanish unconcealed. "And this view will make him feel even the luckier," she says looking out.

The journalist sits slowly and carefully and pours some water from a carafe into an empty glass. He sips conscientiously and feels the water roll down his dry throat.

Stanish touches the journalist's cheek and forehead with the back of his fingers. "He does feel better. Honey, he does feel better, ay. Hey, buddy, do you feel better?"

"I guess," the journalist says, swallowing hard and difficulty.

A waiter comes up and asks the journalist if he would like some coffee. The journalist shakes away the question with his head but points to the tostada and whispers a hoarse, "por favor."

"It is amazing," says Janine staring at the beach. "Yes, it is amazing, it is also amazing you are here, we thought you were dead…thought you had left us. It is lucky those Ohio girls let us crash in their place…I don't know why you didn't like them, they were so nice." She pauses and looks to the journalist who has just begun coughing so intensely that tears come to his eyes. "You slept the whole train ride down here…we practically had to carry you the whole way, it was like the undead." She looks back at the beach. Gulls land and pick dead crab meat from useless shells.

The waiter returns and places a plate of tostada in front of the journalist.

"Hey Honey, look at those gulls, ay. Yeah, just look at 'em," says Stanish as Janine stares in the same direction as he. The journalist picks up the tostada and pecks at it timidly.

BLACKTOP EDEN

IT WAS THEIR DREAM come true—blacktop earth, sprawling six square miles of it. Their paradise. They paid for acres, but no one could remember how many, and they couldn't measure that way anyway. From the center, where Suzy and Amerasian Lilly set their tent, you could look out three miles in each direction, and see nothing but black breaking horizon, the edges of their world folding like the corners of their street dreams. They pooled money and bought the desert, a square of it, and laid this sheet of steaming black diamond down themselves. The fumes coated and ate at your nostrils, like they did the boys' black hands. When Jaime hacked and spit, the glob dangled and swung from her lower lip in the way of Hot Rod's rod as he danced around, naked in the sun. He was saying to her, that's it baby, smell that, take it all in, let us know it is real and working. One day it will all be covered, all of it, Cam Shaft shouts, as he practices sliding across the hood of his GTO in only cutoff jeans and checkered vans. Face down, ass down, back and forth, on either side of his car. It doesn't look like he is even trying to land on his feet; only taste more of that gelling, drying, steaming blackness.

YESTERDAY the boys finished. Last night was celebration. This is flat freedom, this is motor heaven. There were only two speeds and no possessions. Fast and stop and everything free. Amerasian Lilly, skin like yellow suede and twin tower tits rising

99

and falling as she alone took Hot Rod and Cam Shaft in the tent last night. Do you think she can ride a dual jet engine, they asked the others before they went in. And she did. The three without heard the rumbling and roaring from the three within.

THE DAWN POPPED and was bleeding. The blacktop steamed in toxic dew. Cam Shaft and Hot Rod slept it off sore, crusted denims for pillows. But Amerasian Lilly took nothing lying down. After four hours sleep, she had the funny-car four-on-the-floor, tearing new marks where the boys had not been. Suzie had shotgun and screamed high and shrill between pulls of morning Redbull and Spirulina. Into the border of new sun, across the line drawn between shadow black and shining dark, they rode to the edge of their world. The eastern border was on fire. They were Apaches riding a burning Thunderbird. A sun shower. Heat lightning. To the west they saw the glinting. Then it was gone. It was Jaime at the line in the light, stepping back into the dark, coaxing the light back to her. Thirteen gauge nipple rings, aureoles tatted with green scales. Nipple-knobs bursting with surgical steel. Venus flytrap inked labia around six dangling clit hoops. From behind her back she drew the checkered flags and, standing in the sun, flashed out the flickering light by waving the flags across her tits and flytrap. The space between the sisters closed. Shrieking, rumbling, and flags flapping in a gravitational pull. Sisters on the concrete plain. Suzie and Jaime who shared the same parents. Amerasian Lilly and Jaime who shared a bed. And underwear. And bubble gum. And strap-ons. And Suzie. All sisters.

THEY TOLD THE BOYS what the edge was like at dawn. It took dawn courage; the edge was the saddest part of their world. The saddest place for them all. One day there won't be one. One day they will ride over the mountains. With new shocks and struts they will bunny-hop the desert peaks. One day they will be nothing but asphalt ant hills. They dreamed together as they rode. Out between a bloody sky above and black sunshine below.

MEOW, MEOW, this pussy wants to ride, purred Suzy, the youngest, the sweetest, the blondest, the tightest. Every morning, everyone pitched in to lotion her down and up. A cocoa-butter kitty, she smelled like the beach and said fuck you to the sun. On the hood of the GTO, the burning metal was hot from within and without. She danced and purred, threatening the paint with her claws, like a cat on a hot tin roof. White pointy ears on a fuzzy white band held her white hair back. Her little ass wiggled its white tail tight in the white tight body suit. Mad Dogg scratched around the tail and down the crack of her ass and she just meowed and meowed. Down the inner white fishnet thigh he pinched and plucked, rubbing, and she turned on him with claws bared. The big hand smacked her ass and nose before she could react and slid roughly into the car and behind the wheel. You want a ride pussy, I'll give you a ride, he said to her and revved up hard and fierce. Suzy landed on her feet on the asphalt and the others all laughed so hard they pissed and cried.

AMERASIAN LILLY and Jaime were making their tits kiss. Their asses stretched bikini bottoms on the simmering ground and they giggled and writhed. From where Mad Dogg circled and howled, they were just two spots—one honey-yellow and one shoe-leather brown. He could not see the chocolate on chocolate nipples kissing those of pink on green. He knew it was happening, but he didn't care. Neither did Cam Shaft as he grilled the meat. Neither did Hot Rod as he poured beer into the chili and his mouth. Neither did Suzy as she licked her wounds. They were all hungry and amusing themselves. Biding their time. At dusk they would race. The hour of the wolf. When the sky and the road shared one reflection. And the exhaust. Gray on gray on gray.

LESSONS FROM
THE GOOD BOOK

MANY HANDS PASSED OVER, on, and around the Good Book with its embroidered macramé jacket, lifting sentimental antique boxes—of bamboo, teak, and one made of seashells glued into place on cardboard—from their past, dated resting places demarcated in dust, without so much as nudging the Good Book from its very own rectangular plot of polished veneer on the cherry wood end table next to a shadow left by the sofa already gone. Throughout the room, people continued to move themselves and furnishings, as previously happened in all of the other rooms on the floors above and below, and as was happening at the same time about the rest of the main floor. The two rooms, dining and study, at the far west end of the floor were already empty, and forces were converging through the hall, kitchen, and pantry on this most focal of all rooms, with its designation of ancestor worship through memento and after-dinner family time. Busying chatter rumbling low and sporadic, the movers worked around, between, and regardless of the immediate family, their orders coming from a higher council than the individual personal interests of the other sons and daughters of the dearly departed. Maria was in charge, the last born, the once and only baby of the family, whose namesake was the very dearly departed matron herself. She was the tornado that was taking the house down, spinning from room to room and back to rooms she was just in, billowing upstairs and into the basement, everywhere and nowhere with the ticking of her double looped strand of pearls and the clicking of her hard black heels against the chipping glaze of the walnut hardwood floors, blowing orders at the crew of movers that she herself hired, and whispering commands, sweet yet stern, at the loose throng of older siblings that were no match for her fury of professionalism. In the living room, with the bulk of family heritage and antique inheritance, it was obvious that the Good Book, nothing more than an old Bible with a handcrafted jacket, would escape Maria's attention; her main concern being her mother's estate finding its true objectivity in bringing in the greatest financial gain at auction to the heirs of the matron's love and legacy, in only the way a favored daughter could provide. So the Good Book remained there on the end table, undisturbed by the maniacal torrent of the young scavenging among the remains of the old, exactly where two old hands, paper-thin, placed it for the last time two months ago, in the very place those same hands left it every night for years before until two very small, but equally delicate hands, two generations younger, lifted it and slipped with it from the room out into the hall.

Free from the crossing orbits of the other bodies and, as she wrongly hoped, the ever-probing telescopic gaze of her mother, the young lady looked down at the book, filling both of her small hands with its jacket, like old yarn, fitting loosely with wear. The book balanced unsteadily on the palm of her right hand as her left traced with its index finger slowly over the gold strands on the cover spelling the bold words, "Family Bible." The first word was all she was able to trace before her mother called, but it was this word that mattered most to her, causing a heart tightening pang stoking the loss of her grandmother and a feeling that with her went her only true feminine familial connection.

"Lucia, what are you looking at out there," rang out her mother's voice from the living room, as if she was watching through the walls, tracking all that she surveyed.

"It's Noni's Bible, Mama," she called out without even looking up, her eyes down on the book. And that is all it took for it to be hers. Maria responded with an okay and some words to the effect of staying out of the way unless she wanted to help, and Lucia replied in an affirmative grunt familiar to parents of adolescents. With chaos a wall away and an eerie stillness above and to the west, she was captivated in the middle by the mystery of this book which, though cherished and revered by many like her grandmother, was a thing of no value to her mother who was always ready to squeeze pennies of posterity from any trinket or bauble hidden under dust. Bibles were a dime a dozen to Maria for the value was inside, locked to some, and it was for that very reason that the deceased treasured this one and put such care into its covering, which the two gentle hands of the young lady now held with care compounded by awe.

Quick, as if making a leap from a precipice over a drop far uncertain to no familiar point of landing, those two hands, too small for their age, angled the Good Book and let it fall open, the weight of pages from the middle pushing each cover out and down in both directions, instigated by an awkward place-marker stuck at the beginning of the *Song of Songs*. Her eyes, sharp like her mother's, made out for a second a fragment of an image from the place-marker before a panic shot through her, holding her breath, speeding and tightening her heart, bursting hot, prickly pink flowers about her cheeks, and causing her to slam the book shut and run out to the backseat of her mother's car.

✳

INTO THE HOUSE Lucia ran when her father opened the door to

greet his women, returning from a process that he supposed was not without a good deal of sadness, and so he did not attempt to stop his daughter in her hurry by him and up the stairs with a large book clutched to her chest, long frizzy brown hair trailing like a comet's tail. Using equal understanding with which he allowed his daughter at her temperamental age to blow by him without so much as a hello, he was also able to greet his wife's prideful countenance as she approached with a mouth ready to complain of the inefficiency of others regardless of their pain or bereavement. They paused for a moment as the loud and resonant sounding of wood on wood slammed down to them, signifying Lucia's presence in the isolated confines of her bedroom.

She had only peeked quickly once more into the book at its place-marker during the course of the ride home, to the same result of flush cheeks and skipping, quickening pulse. She rode in the back, and up front her mother noticed nothing. Now, on her bed, she sat with the book on her denim lap, her back straight and aware from nervousness. She wiped her palms with hot friction down the legs of her jeans, clearing the moisture beading there. All the while, she could not take her eyes off the book, staring through the golden words in splintering cords at the exposed corner of a mystery that lies beneath. She was pretty sure of what she saw and she was curious to see more.

Lucia took a breath and tried to slow her heart in preparation, but in thinking of for what she prepared it, it sped even faster. She had no choice. The leap was made; as if to absolve some responsibility and letting gravity work to Fate's end she stood the book on its spine in the gully between her thighs and allowed it to fall open on her lap. In that now familiar and most likely of ways it fell, chapter one of the *Song of Songs* with a thick age-browned piece of paper standing upright, its edge tight in the cleavage of the soft thin pages, like a flag marking secret treasure.

In a moment of small victory, she pulled the place-marker from the binding's grip and laid it down on the right page, the first page of the *Song of Songs* to the left. It was a photograph and its face was up to her. Lucia breathed again. The sepia tone of the image and the beaten wear of the paper hearkened back to a period surrounding Time's gentle roll from the nineteenth into the twentieth century. She looked at the photograph hard, not so much the format now, but finally the image itself, as the square form of it teetered on the soft Bible pages, like thin old skin, with its bent edges and creased corners shifting to the new air finally free from the Good Book's control.

As Lucia looked at the picture for a piece of time that lingered with a kiss over the hand of Infinity, fated for nothing more than a courteous kiss, everything seemed to fade away and subside to still and quiet. Within the frame of the photograph's border was the awkwardly erect naked body of a woman straddling the lap of a man, his bare legs jutting out between hers, his penis inside of her, the rest of him gone forever behind her back. She did not notice that her heart had slowed and the beats hung in the air over the intervals till the one that followed bumped out. The palms of her hands dried to the cool air in her room as they hung by thumbs from the yarn covered edges of the book cover. Her whole face and forehead and all her exposed skin cooled too, and a general de-contraction happened to all the muscles of her body. Her mouth went dry and her tongue lay still against her hidden under-bite. Lucia's eyes took in the picture, tracing it, scanning it. From top to bottom, the way the woman's hair was up on her head, her arms up with her hands hidden behind her bun of hair, her distant eyes, her mysterious smile, the cocking of her neck, the hang of her breasts with dark nipples, the strips of dark armpit hair, the elongation of the abdomen down the outward push of the stomach to the dark hair and the partial penis, the four legs, two dark with hair and the others lighter and fair, the four feet, two flat and the others taut and gripping for balance, Lucia took the picture in. She got to the point of wondering what it was that the man was laying on, since the room within the picture's frame was dark and nondescript, but her peace reached its predestined end when her mother called for her attendance at dinner.

With the invasion of that alien voice into the seclusion of her room, and more so the precarious intent of her focus, a shock shot through her, generating fear and guilt and their required expression in heartbeat, sweat, and muscle contractions. The Good Book slammed shut quicker than she could think and she pushed it under her pillows. She shot up from the bed smoothing and fixing nervously, perceiving herself as disheveled.

✳

"But she was my mother!"

"Well, yes, and she was their mother too. Actually she was all of their mother longer, since you are the youngest."

"What does that matter? It's not the years, it's the miles that make the difference. She meant something different to me."

"You can't say that. How do you know how they feel? Everyone expresses love differently."

"It's in their actions. I showed my appreciation greater. I lived my appreciation. If you love something, you show it; you act it. That love becomes part of who you are. Since her death, I haven't even stopped. I will not go moping about and let her estate be less than what she made it."

"I don't think that she cared too much about the value of her possessions outside of their sentimental value."

"That's not the point, she needs to be done right by in her death and it seems like there is only me to do it. Like I did when she was alive. What did those others do, those deadbeats, a card at Christmas with a picture of their kid? They showed off their kids to gain more favoritism, and get more money out of her. And now they think they can all pick and poke around the house and all her stuff and just take what they want? Where were they last year after she got out of the hospital when the bill came? I paid it. And when the funeral costs came in August? You know where that came from. So who do you think should be taking care of all this?"

"Well, you of course, Dear. I know what you've been through. I went through it all with you. I loved Noni, too. It just sounds like you are concentrating on the money and that your love for her was an investment."

"Well…it was an investment. It was an investment of love. I put in a lot of love and she gave a lot back. I felt her love and I felt it was stronger for me than for the others because I deserved it, it wasn't simple biology. And it became a monetary investment too, and there is nothing wrong with that, and for me to get the greatest return and even a bigger return for those others than they deserve, I should handle it all. I am the most qualified, anyway."

"There is no doubt about that. This is just a hard time for us all and I would just like to make sure your heart is in the right place, not saying that it isn't, but it is always good to hear it from you"

And they went on like this for most of the meal across the table from end to end and poor Lucia, sitting on one side to the right of mother, felt like she was in the corner of a room filled only by their one-sided bombast and banter, which she had learned to tune out. She did not always ignore what they were saying, but it seemed they spoke on without even trying to include her, and her only recourse was to retaliate painfully with the lie that she didn't care if they did or not. There was no neglect under the eye of her mother, though, on the surface.

"Young lady," she turned sharply from her response to her husband to rear on her daughter, "you're slouching. Do you want a hump? Do you think there is a market at circuses and carnivals for Italian-Jewish hunchbacks?"

Lucia's annoyance and hurt let out a pout painfully below what she thought appropriate of her age group.

"Maria," a hushed snap of a man feigning authority went from David to his wife.

"Young Lady, please, shoulders back, neck straight, chest out, and I want to be able to feel the arch of your back between you and the chair."

Lucia moved into this position with displayed reluctance. As she moved and felt the awkwardness of this way of sitting, she pictured the woman in the photograph in the Bible and the erectness of her back. She held it all for a few minutes, her thoughts, the position. The association, blossoming hot pink flowers about her cheeks, brought guilt and the anxiety brought a little nausea. She felt that they knew what she was thinking, thought they'd notice her cheeks, but her parents were back to talking, her father telling of his day at his orthodontic office and her mother turning the conversation back to her ungrateful siblings and their jealousy of the way she lives. Lucia excused herself and ran to the bathroom.

✳

Let him kiss me with kisses of his mouth…the king hath brought me into his chambers…and he shall lie all night betwixt my breasts… She vowed not to open the Good Book again that night. It had remained under her pillow, causing a foolish bulge and offsetting the symmetry and order that the left pillow helped maintain for the rest of the bed. But here she was reading. It wasn't until she was undressed and redressed, brushed, flossed, washed of face, and ready for bed that she had to deal with the self-prohibited obstacle beneath the pillow. In she slid, between her duvet and soft flannel sheets, placing her head on the flat pillow and resting her hand on the top of the skewed pillow. With the gradual breakdown of discipline, she traced on the pillow the rectangular shape beneath, feeling the hidden pea like only the most sensitive princess could. Easily she dragged the book out and propped herself up on her right elbow, opening the book to the marked page and reading on the left side, letting the photograph expose itself up to her on the right. She fought to ignore the picture and gradually began to win, given over to the text.

...*Kisses of his mouth...betwixt my breasts*...Lucia had never heard of the *Song of Songs* and was amazed that this was in the Bible. She only read the first couple chapters, wanting to continue but not wanting to look to her right, to the right page, where the picture was. From the influence of her mother, she dabbled in self-discipline, and now she fought to hold her ground against a rising lust. So, in staving off the temptation, she focused on the words before her—not so much the story, which she could not follow past its beginning, but the snippets of words and phrases that stood out to her, fueling further the mystery of the story it told.

Though excited in some ways, a drowse crept across Lucia, certain new phrases now stood out under her wandering, yet concentrated, eye...*Oh ye daughters of Jerusalem...I am black because the sun hath looked upon me...I have compared the, Oh my love, to a company of horses*...She was in some way a daughter of Jerusalem, her sleepy mind mused. Her elbow and right hand ached beneath her head, as from its straight focus she shifted her gaze to look down to her chest in the loose collar of her tank top. The soft, young skin is pale, she is not black. The limited sun effects from the summer faded fast over the last month or so, and below the tan line no effects were registered. Her left breast, about the size of her small left fist, leans archingly down to barely touch the right, smooshed by the bed and bulging in a way to give the illusion of greater mass. The Bible stayed open as she slid her left hand from the yarn edge and felt the thin gentle flesh over her sternum and down into the space between her breasts, under the arch of the left breast...*And he shall lie all night betwixt my breasts... I have compared thee, Oh my love, to a company of horses...*The conflict of imagery dreamily created exciting discord, her left hand's fingers tracing up across the top of her small left breast, her eyes darting with reflexive celerity to the photograph. Lucia's whole body heated up and the pink flowers familiar to her cheeks went red. She reached out and slammed the Good Book pushing it about an inch away, a statement of her new distance, while a maculopapular flush broke out about her chest and the top of her breasts. She rolled over onto her left side, stretching the cramp out of her right arm and turning out the lamplight at the same time, her right ear matching the heat of the rest of her body from where her hand pressed against it.

In the darkness, her body was quick to cool and soon she was asleep. After a short time Lucia rolled over back onto her right side and her left hand fell onto the soft, macramé cover of the Good Book in bed beside her.

✳

THE OCTOBER WIND swept down the suburban streets and sidewalks with its gusts of lawn dust and debris and its whirls of leaves and pine-straw equally disrespectful of motorists and pedestrians alike, the former with their needs of visibility in reading signs and lines and the latter getting blinded and splintered in mere pursuit of exercise. A harbinger of autumnal splendor, they decorate while dancing and whipping to and fro, hither and thither with the myriad colors the season denotes, from browns of brittle decay to greens bright like ripening fruit and in between, reds ranging from rust to fire, yellows from sunlight to lemon, and all the shades and degrees created by the layering of hues in fallen foliage completing their life cycle. Nature's play with color creates new life in a season that would otherwise seem to be a last hurrah before the frightful monochrome of winter, and this play is in a way new life itself at a time of harvest; the joy behind the colorful artistry melding with the joyous sounds of children at play in piles of Nature's very swatches of color. Mid-October is the autumnal pinnacle, as one is unable to deny the advent of winter in the chill of the air but that chill is not yet as bitter as November brings, with its thinner, darker foliage and early dusk, and how the last days of September's Indian Summer still warm the memory with daylight savings time a week off the horizon.

Before the five o'clock hour of a weekday, this upscale residential neighborhood rests serenely undisturbed, with only the movement of the occasional housewife running home between a lunch engagement and either the last opportunities for tennis of the season or to pick the younger children up from half-day preschool, or maybe even to drive the maid to the train station. For most children the school day ended before four, but the school bus does not make it to this street until about four thirty and those rare students who ride the afternoon bus, a group which excludes those with after-school programs and activities, have not returned home yet to disturb this quiet street. At this time the champagne SUV, adding another earth tone into the general sienna of the day, of Maria Merkowitz pulls up in front of the house purchased mutually by herself and her husband, Dr. Merkowitz, to sit at an idle with the engine running and discard a passenger who neither took the bus nor attended after-school programs or activities.

Lucia's parents, with the best of intentions, thought of her as shy and she let them. They did not push her to do the things that they did as adolescents or things they heard of other children doing these days, mostly shying away from the issues of adjustment while attempting to leave her room to breath in her first year of high school.

"Don't go out anywhere until your father gets home, which shouldn't be till around six-thirty. I'll be home by dinnertime," came from the car as the passenger door opened and the slight teenaged girl stepped out of it, slinging a purple backpack over her left shoulder with the corresponding hand, carrying a plastic pharmacy bag wrapped tightly around a cardboard box in her right, before the door slammed shut, allowing the car to roll away, and she ran to the house. On the porch she held the glass storm door, which wheezed out like a tired old friend, with her right foot, and fumbled for her house key in her backpack with her left hand, feeling about for the stuffed purple monkey key-chain. Immediately upon entrance she hung up her black overcoat and started turning on all the lights that she passed, a home alone precaution instilled by her mother, making her way up the stairs of the split-level ranch home to her bedroom, the only thing on that floor besides a bathroom.

The purple backpack sailed smoothly into her bedroom, landing at the foot of the bed, the rest of Lucia turning and gone within the bathroom entrance directly across the hall. A new light is thrown from the bathroom out into the hall, followed by an orange and white striped shirt, the left beige shoe, then the right, flared blue jeans, socks with stripes of peach, yellow, pink and violet of different widths, flying in a balled clump, and after a short amount of time, a small white bra with orange flowers slings by, landing on top of the loose clump made by its predecessors on Lucia's bed. The sound of the shower nozzle bursting forth with water could be heard around the house, through the door that the young girl shut and locked with care, the only sound in a pristine home, empty and clean, with only a modicum of dust glinting in the setting sunlight, filtered like gold through mustard yellow drapes, and only the movement of moisture in the air, rushing and diffusing, motivated by heat.

✳

LUCIA stepped from the shower into the embrace of her big, fluffy, white bath towel. She dried herself and pulled the stopper on the sink so as to drain the water in which her panties were soaking, ringing them out and looking to survey the damage before hanging them to dry clandestinely on the towel rod under her face cloth. Rust-brown, brick-red stains clung to where their flow subsided and dried and where they will always remain, on the outer thin crotch strip of the small underpants, blending lighter between the flowers once orange and darker over those flowers now like rust. The damage was already done by the time she noticed what was happening during a restroom break between second and third periods, but with the presence of her backpack she was as prepared for such an incident as she had been for the last four months.

Occurring early last June, a week before her fourteenth birthday and days before the end of the school year—her last year of Middle School, and in some respects, childhood— her menarche proved nothing less than a private torture of awkwardness, fear, and embarrassment. It was during the final assembly, somewhat likened to a Middle School graduation, where Lucia sat listening to the names of student award recipients. During the announcement of the winners for Perfect Attendance, she felt a warm trickling sensation like urine move and stir under the upper part of her thighs and rear end against her seat. She couldn't feel her bladder, it was not as if she was peeing, but it was something uncertain and, for those moments that felt like Eternity, she was scared and wanted to cry, praying to God that they would not call her name to get up for an award, even though she clearly knew that she could not possibly be a prospect for the Perfect Attendance Award after the time she spent with her mother taking care of her Noni in the hospital a half dozen months before.

Through the remaining names she sat and through the closing speech—where the principal welcomed the students in saying goodbye to a chapter in the book of their lives that was ending only to allow another to begin that can be just as bright and rewarding—she still sat, clenching her jaw, cheeks rose red with fear, with ears as hot as her palms were wet, concentrating on the mystery trickling and spreading between her flesh and her seat, not ignorant to its cause, yet not yet relieved by her suspicion. And when it all was over, she stared into her Social Studies text book open on her lap, eyes down, intent, as if in search for the answers to last night's homework or in last minute study for next period's final exam, all the while waiting for everyone in her row to shuffle out and then everyone in the two rows surrounding her before she stood. Shaped like the island of Greenland from the world map on the cover of Lucia's Social Studies textbook, lay a brown quick-drying island of blood on the white fabric of her seat. An image of the island's twin emblazoned the back of Lucia's white skirt almost crimson in the florescent light of the school's auditorium. The immediacy of no other person did not prevent poor Lucia from an edgy paranoia and regardless of how natural she knew this to be and how most girls she knew already menstruated on a regular cycle she could not resist the temptation to hide the evidence and runaway. A tact that was easily a product of her mother's undying sense of decorum caused her to pause for a moment and place her Social Studies textbook on the seat before slinging her backpack behind her, covering her backside and running stealthily behind the other children to the buses. That evening after school, her mother took her out and bought her a box of tampons. They were pink with flowers on the box. After a few days when the bleeding stopped, Lucia put the last remaining tampon in her backpack and took it with her everywhere she went.

Today when Nature struck, with its slippery lunar reminder of budding womanhood and the trappings of cyclicality, she was prepared, and this preparation permeated to such an emotional level that Lucia called her mother to be picked up from school with the intention of further demonstrating her security in the form of a mother/daughter pharmacy adventure. Maria Merkowitz allowed the unscheduled divergence from her appointments showing model homes, something rarely allowed, she being the judge of what deemed the status "Emergency" in her well-run family, and embraced her daughter's cry for assistance as a welcomed compliment for her aptitude of mothering and capabilities of nurturing. The result of Mrs. Merkowitz's matronly proficiency sat in a plastic bag in front of the mirror and next to the bathroom sink, its potential undisturbed while Lucia dried her hair. The bag went into the trash and the box, opened and closed without any more than the most calm and gentle extraction of one item of its contents, went quaintly into the cabinet beneath the sink in a bare space between a handed down set of hot curlers from her older cousin Tracy and an unused first aid kit. After the plastic wrapper landed upon the plastic bag in the trash, Lucia continued with her calm, cleansed, fresh feeling from the shower and moved slowly, assuring herself this would be an easier process than earlier in the school bathroom with the older girls talking and her distorted reflection thrown back at her from the cold shiny metal of the stall. Here in the crystal cleanliness of her bathroom she was safe and standing naked, except for the fluffy towel tower on her head. She allowed her knees to loosen and veer further apart while her hands went to work with unhurried efficiency; to wince and look away, she put her eyes upward and saw herself in the mirror and for a moment it was ugly and in the next moment she looked further up to look herself in the eyes, a look that reassured her into looking more, and in doing so she saw in her squatting and contracted shape the woman in the photography, a grown woman, a sexual woman, far more womanly than her, with her slight pale breasts and sparse pubic growth, but amidst this intense act Lucia understood that they were essentially the same and of the same capabilities, and this understanding brought a sharp terror with its excitement so as she pulled the applicator out, she looked ceiling-ward to see no more.

✳

THE SECOND DAY of Lucia's second menses was a dull stroll of routine compared to the first day of her second menses which, in its own right, regardless of its mnemonic freshness and distinct note of realized maturity, could neither enter any competition nor warrant any comparison with that first day of her first menses. It being a Thursday meant that the daughter of Mr. and Mrs. Merkowitz was alone while her parents worked late, as they did Wednesday, Tuesday, and Monday, drilling teeth and showing homes, leaving Fridays open for the early jump on the weekend ordeal of searching for family time amongst errands, shopping, dry-cleaning drop off and pick-up, last minute open houses, emergency root canals, garage sales, some cousin's birthday at a roller rink or miniature golf range, and whatever other ephemeral obligation of social existence undulated insistently upon their horizon. This unsupervised time Lucia sanctioned for homework, while her parents arrested any guilt or worry with the supposition that their daughter was safely watching television, which allowed the clever child to use the post-dinner time of the evening, with its official parental designation for study, to do as she liked in her room without parental prying eyes or words. She forgave herself this deception since it still allowed her to complete the day's homework requirements while the private time she gained in forfeit of television watching was spent at innocent pursuits.

Since Sunday and the advent of her grandmother's Good Book, the reward of bearing false witness to the parents whose trust she bears has been the meticulous exploration of the secret photograph that she believed would elicit condemnation from her parents, along with the occasional reading from a passage at random of the *Song of Songs*, which she felt had a more refined air of taboo. The fact that, along with the Book, the photograph was also a possession of her late grandmother alleviated some of the guilt in a deception damned further by taboo.

Early in the week Lucia wondered if maybe the woman in the photograph was her grandmother, a prospect that stirred more nausea in her than curiosity, along with a guilt and a sadness over her grandmother's death, but that notion was resolved by a fourteen year old deductive reasoning, estimating that the picture was taken about the turn of the century, the sepia reminding her of scenes from an old western she watched once with her father, so it was far too old to be a representation of her grandmother. No, the picture was special to her grandmother for some other reason, and this drew her expanding awareness further into not only the photograph itself, but the enigma of from where it was unearthed.

Lucia can go back to many memories just like last Christmas, Noni on the sofa of the dimly lit family room, the throw she just finished knitting across her shoulders after a dinner with family and their extensions, the dying light a haze radiating her through the window to her left and, regardless of the swirling cacophony produced by two dozen relatives spanning five months to fifty years of age at siege upon the silent history of the cluttered room, she remains serene with the Good Book in her lap, her fingers gently playing with the loose strands of its macramé cover. Or when, as a child, her parents left her in the care of her grandmother and Lucia, on the floor coloring quietly, would notice Noni with the Book in her lap, reading silently from its large, thin pages. Through these memories, now x-rayed by her awareness of the hidden photograph, Lucia began to see her grandmother as more than just a grandmother, as a woman; a being complicit in what she saw in her mirror image yesterday and what of herself she saw in the photograph every night before she closed the light to sleep. She felt like she knew her grandmother better now in death than she was ever permitted to in life. With a wisdom beyond her generous baker's dozen of years, Lucia suspected, but could not yet grasp why, that *Song of Songs* built round-about roads of metaphor and dark alleyways of imagery to distract and delay, with zigzags of philosophy probing like headlights into the green-hedged human heart, through a pastoral storyboard of love in triangulation; while all the while at its barest, basest, depth and core its message could be as efficiently and bluntly expressed with the action depicted within the bent edges of the photograph, browned under the chronic abuses of Atmosphere and curiosity.

✳

A STRENGTH of character—in one turn hardened by a mother's love and honed with a Warrior's business acumen and assertiveness and in another softened with the equally Warrior-like power to bend and yield, derived from an older, deeper matriarchal heredity and inspiration—expressed itself in an exemplary vow of discipline last Monday while Lucia ran her second lap around the high school's track during fourth period, Physical Education. At that moment of physical fortitude and strength, fueled by one complete lap at pace with the class's fastest, the slight young girl made a decision that if she were to engage any further into the perusal of the antique photograph, which at once scared and enticed her last night in bed, beyond the knowledge of her parental guardians and any other living soul, then she must be smart and her actions consistent. No more sneaked peeks like the one this morning post-shower at any time throughout the day except during the allotted time in the confines and safety of her room before bedtime.

The righteous steadfastness and commitment with which she purged her desire and deprived her curiosity, keeping the Good Book and its contents only in the smallest corner of her dreamy hormonal cerebellum, lead her easily to binge on the preplanned daily routine of school and home life. The repetitive actions appeased all parental concerns—where they expected her to be she was; there was no need to look for her, so they didn't. Both consumed with their own lives, but with an overflow of consumption from Mrs. Merkowitz's life into her husband's, they could find no fault with their daughter's anti-social behavior. And, whether an act of cowardice, fear, faith, or mature parenting, they let her grow, for the most part, unfettered. This did not mean that the gentle daughter was free from the stern mother's commands, criticisms, and cutting comments— those she could suffer worse than any other. It only meant that out of sight, in her room, she was on her own; and besides, they thought she was studying.

For Lucia Merkowitz, her nightly ritual was a form of study. And religious study was the outward appearance of the young girl sitting bolt upright with a large Bible on her lap, tense and intent, in the sanctuary of her room at a time of evening when other girls might be out with their friends or watching television with their family. Devoted and penitent, with head bowed over the tome, she sought within the Good Book not its words, but its content, or more precisely its contents, for the silky tissue pages lined and blocked with words and numbers, some bold and some italicized, made a liturgical frame for the golden, honey-brown representation of physical love. Her exegesis was not textual, but pictorial, and from Monday on, her posture gradually relaxed, easing into a greater freedom of movement and physical intimacy with the Good Book and its contents, while her gaze and eye of scrutiny honed in, contracted and more intense, plumbing deeper into the depths of the fading image. Her relaxing form, a vessel given over to purpose, allowed the action captured on photographic paper to develop and reveal itself while her eye, voracious in appetite after a day of restraint and desire, took a mile of understanding and imagination from each inch of revelation.

Structure and order will always prevail in any endeavor, great or small, taken by a girl of such sensibility as young Lucia, and verily each night of biblical study had within itself its own parameters, control, and limitations.

Monday night her ravenous eyes, after a day of minimal deprivation, disciplined nonetheless, scanned in blurry sweeps from corner to corner up and down and back across, washing over the image, never quite focusing on any particular part, allowing limbs and form, connections and expression, to blend into an exciting and chaotic visual soup stirred in her agitation and the general sepia tone. In her lap the Good Book spread itself, each half weighing like a stone tablet on the red flannel pajama pants over each leg, with the photo floating over the parting of the spread pages of text while her neck, curved out and down so her eyes could look straight down in their study, tightened to a slight crick. The feast was short-lived, a smorgasbord of sensory material filling the innocent and small girl rapidly on tastes diverse and unfocused, yet for no longer than twenty minutes. Her resolve to cease and sleep was quick to vow, followed by instant reluctance and a desire to look once more, just once more, before she turns out the light; already under the covers, the fingers from her left hand already on the lamp switch as she looked across her body at the gold and white yarn cover of the Good Book, lying on its half of the bed like a taunting sleep-over companion not yet ready for bed.

Tuesday was calmer, the Good Book and its photograph more familiar and somewhat lighter in Lucia's hands after she scrubbed her face, brushed her teeth, changed into her pajama bottoms and a loose tank top, and quickly ran to lay with open covers on her fluffy bed as if she were curling up with an enjoyable piece of required reading; so it was here that her examination reached a point of particular depth. With parameters previously established during the evening meal, watching her own wandering thoughts lead sneakily back to her biblical exercises, though hinted at and lured to earlier in the day's course, she set out to start in the most textbook way, at the top. No longer glancing and darting, eluding by scanning, the young penitent eyes, wiser by the day, focused in, but only to the isolated area of the photo's top half, and the top half of the woman it bore. Only in awareness of her own body could she take in the body of the Other. The triangulation established in top corners by the woman's elbows lead down to a point at the bust line, where Lucia kept finding her own eyes, noticing the way the breasts of the Other with small dark nipple-circles hung with slight shadowing beneath them. Within her loose tank top, her young budding bosom pointed out straight with little hang, scraping their thin covering with areolas pale as the rest of their mass, while she knew from experience that if she were to lift her arms in such a way the small masses themselves would tighten to almost retraction.

Lucia's eyes remained within the established boundary above the abdomen and, after her initial interest in the breasts, attractive in their well-formed differences from her own, yet easy to ascertain in their intrinsic similarity, her main visual stimulation lay in the look forever cast upon the framed woman's face. The arms were slender and plain, the hair in a loose and tousled bun hiding the hands, the armpits darkly striped with hair, adding to her period-piece mystique, and even all together their only appeal seem to be the framing of that face, arched back into the room's bare overhead light source by her long cocked neck. Face to face with the Other, Lucia fell to reclining with her head remaining erect, her body literally curled up around the work. Only the tension in her neck and her locked gaze still represented the ascetic at study, her body comfortable with itself and the activity. Above and below the pert, incidental nose that she could almost see up lay the equally primary causes of Lucia's wonder. Whether the woman was actually smiling, along with a question of towards what did the woman's eyes look, became the catechism Lucia's cunning mind inflicted upon her. Spread ever so slightly with the faintest hint of dimpling at their corners, the lips were only cracked enough to let out a wisp of breath between her two front gapped top teeth. The eyes were thrown back in their sockets in the same manner the head was thrown back on its neck, their pupils at their limits of visibility, wide in the path of the light source, light sliding across her face, somewhat reminiscent of Bernini's Saint Theresa, but with eyes open. For her understanding of this look was like a word at the tip of her tongue somewhere deep within her memory. She thought this look to be ecstasy, but that word did not roll from her tongue with the understanding she thought it should. Lucia's puzzlement was countered by the daily increasing sense of routine attached to her evening study and within her relaxing body, drawn to slumber by Night's rising Moon, a tense opposition lay in the wake of that dark and exciting picture that she chose to ignore in order to turn out the light and sleep.

Wednesday bore a sense of coincidence so obvious between the overdue arrival of her second menses and the lower-half focus of the day's lesson plan that it was even noticed with Lucia's dry, wry sense of humor. Before retiring to study time behind the closed door of her bedroom with an anxious and embarrassed acknowledgment of what she was to be examining tonight, she went to the bathroom and replaced her tampon, realizing it was already her third today, wondering if that was safe, if that was normal, yet preceding to feel clean and therefore comfortable. The operation of application was swifter with her tertiary attempt and in preparation for the detail of her biblical study, she allowed her view to linger upon the light brown ridge of her pubic bone. Then in her room, she positioned herself to sit upright with her back against her pillows and her legs under the covers of her bed. The Good Book was separated from her lap by the thickness of duvet and sheets. When it was opened she tried to dance around the photograph by reading text, her eyes creeping outside of the picture's borders, grabbing random words of biblical script *exult…love…vineyard…*but getting too hot and flowery of cheek and nerves, her vision glazing over to a hazing blur of words till she gave up all hope and threw her eyes down at the feet of the man half ghost. His feet were flat of the ground with hairy calves close together that went up to knees leading back to nothing. From the genitals she brought her view back down to the feet of the woman, for all that remained of the man was his penis, behind the woman was the darkness cast by shadow. Her legs were hairless, or of pale hair, and from her taut toes gripping at the floor, they led up to her full hips. Subtly avoiding the genitals again, she focused on the long abdomen of the Other, with a hang more gradual than that of the breasts above, but fuller than her own, pushing out and down to a hairline almost black, as if the Other was sitting relaxed and comfortable.

Lucia felt that her legs were sweating beneath the covering sheets and duvet and Good Book, the beads casting-off against the red flannel pajama bottoms as she remained still. Lifting the Book by its soft stringy edges, she tented her knees and kicked at her covers until they were removed and piled at the bed's foot. Laying her legs down on the bare bottom sheet to cool, she took the momentary distraction as an opportune chance to dive unrestrained by thought into the center of the picture's action. At the direct connection of the man and woman, the unfamiliar parts abstracted in such close inspection, the uneducated eyes of Miss Merkowitz widened their focus and rested on the whole area. Lucia had learned all of the technical names for what she now saw in health class three years ago and used them in the description she gave herself mentally of what she found before her in the lower center of the antique photograph resting in the middle of the soft white expanse of Bible, speckled with tiny black illegible words. She knew other terms, terms boys used mostly, terms she heard in movies and from girls that other girls whispered about. Words like those held no place in her study—the picture and what it entailed were sanctified by the biblical casing and the memory of her sweet grandmother. The act being performed before her eyes and through her technical narration was mature and holy, and in her sense of respect and awe she felt herself touching both holiness and maturity. The mental control with which she described to herself what she saw helped harness the physical symptoms resulting from her exposition; the increasing sweat beneath the flannel pants, especially where the excess bunched up around the thin girl's inner thigh, and the light trickle falling from her shaven armpits against her rigid arms with hands locked on the Good Book's loose edges.

A heat permeated her flesh ubiquitously and while describing to herself the way that the man's penis was lost within the woman's vaginal opening for the umpteenth time, Lucia found herself with a heightened awareness of the tampon inside her own vagina. She wondered if that difficulty of application was present in the sex act or does the difference between plastic and skin make all the difference. It frightened her, the size of the penis and the greatness of the woman's opening, and she continued to assume that the woman was just built big and therefore just right for the size of the man. She dared not look now, but thought about how only a half of an hour before she saw the white string dangle from her as if it were a penis, though far smaller than that of the Other, which she was looking at. A penis the size of the white string would be best for her if when it stood up it was the size of the tampon, which did not bother her inside, though its presence was noticeable. She did not understand from just looking at the genitals in the picture how the result could be pleasure when she only underwent stress in the application of her feminine product, which resulted in pretty much what she saw in this half of the picture, and she found herself far more excited by the image itself than the tampon and its placement. Exhausted in her scrutiny, body temperature, and heightened self-awareness, Lucia closed the Good Book and the light on her night and lay in the darkness cooling, fading to sleep with the sweaty yarn cover inches from her flesh.

Thursday was traversed with minimal effort and a far more relaxed awkwardness within her own hormonally brimming body until evening when Lucia noticed its contrast in a feeling of dread and confusion around the normal anxious excitement of her nightly lesson. She thought clearly inside of her routines, and as she washed her face, scrubbing in prevention of creepingly inevitable acne, her wavy brown hair, tight back in a doubled over ponytail, except for the frizzies getting wet with her forehead, the warm water splashing against her face and falling and rising up again as steam opening her pores, she wondered what was left to plumb from the picture. She knew all of its details, she knew what action it held and what story it told and now she was left to face it on terms with herself. No longer was the photograph itself a mystery, but it was still an excitement and she suspected, not without worry, what new mystery awaited her. The face cloth was returned to the horizontal rod beside the mirror after she rinsed thoroughly and fluffed it against her face until dry. The fourteen-year old girl then trudged dutifully into her own bedroom in a manner comparable to that of a lamb to slaughter and laid her sacrificial form down within the covers of her bed, staring sheepishly down at the Good Book with embroidered macramé jacket spelling out "Family Bible" in gold strands.

Lucia, laying on her left side, elevated the book to stand on its spine and it fell open from the middle in its faithful way, parted at the first chapter of *Song of Songs* by a place-marker that was snatched free by her quick right hand, before knocking the Book back closed with her left. The faded brown ancient photograph free, the young lady pushed the Good Book to the edge of the bed and rolled away from it onto her right side. Lying on her side, she held the old photograph in her hand by its corner, reviewing what she knew about it, reviewing her studies. The arms, the hidden hands, the breasts, the nipples, the stomach, the pubic hair, the intercourse, the penis, the two tones of legs and feet; all of it she was familiar with, all of it she grew to understand as she grew familiar with different parts, older parts, bigger parts, more developed parts and even masculine parts, but something still generated confusion. The lesson of Tuesday ended on a note that echoed through Lucia and she reached again for a word of understanding in endeavoring to relate to the face of the woman depicted in the photograph. She slid herself down her bed a few inches and pulled with her free hand one of her pillows down beneath her back and swiveled her shoulders flat while her legs remained curled to the right. Facing resistance she hoisted and discarded her tank top and lay back against her pillow, turning her neck in line with her left shoulder and looking up and left to the only lamp bright in her room. She returned her strained neck forward and her eyes to the picture and wondered if there was any pain in the woman's neck while she waited for the photographer to take the picture. It was the first thought she had of the photographer responsible for the picture, but she let that lesson slip away for another day as the lesson plan of present caught up all her active attention. Shaking the tightness out of her own neck Lucia swiveled her hips to lay flat and while she studied the composition of the woman inside the picture's four sides, her free hand brought down her red flannel pajama pants and fresh white underpants in one swift thoughtless move. With an arch of her back she made a bridge from her shoulders against the pillow to her bare rear end, all the while her eyes read the picture from the Good Book, like an actor reading blocking, and she extended her toes, gripping at the sheet with her legs spread just so. Lucia sent her free right hand through the thickness of her thin undergrowth, parting and drawing up the white string straight against her, like its photographic equivalent, and took one last look at the picture before releasing it to look up over her shoulder at the lamp light, her mouth cracked in a smile with a wisp of breath escaping around and between her gapped front teeth. It was here that Lucia Merkowitz realized and understood, as her left hand hid behind her tousled mass of hair and her right tightened its gentle grip below, that the expression upon the rapturous woman's face, burned within that fading sepia photograph, was one of victory.

ACKNOWLEDGEMENTS

THERE ARE SO MANY PEOPLE TO THANK who read these stories along the way and never once told me I was a complete idiot for continuing at this work (though some did give me sly glances and side-eye). Also, if anyone finds a personal likeness to any character in these stories that is purely coincidental, I am the sole god and creator of the personae here within. Here is a list of those that have kept, and continue to keep, me going, early readers, friends, and family: Tanya Pina, Melissa Leahy, Adam Shprintzen, Caroline Conzatti, Julianna Tozzi, Carlos Santiago, Okla Elliott, Daniel and Tiffany Chameides (and Elijah), Ariane and Clint (and John and Catherine), Dad and Jody, West Price, Gail Polk, Jon Polk and Emily (and Ada), Travis and Susie, Brian and Anna Grace (and Greta), William and Crystal Brandon (and Quentin and Greyson), Liz Cunningham, Mark Hewitt, Micheal Karczewski, Michael Petri, Adrienne and Amy Gandolfi, Neil Graf, Kai Reidl, Jeremy Ayers, Molly Williams, Curtis Vorda, Raymond Langley, Reginald McKnight, Mark Hewitt, Lazarus Roth, Ian Campbell, Nick and Erin Mauldin, Faisal Khan, and William T. Vollmann.

AND MOST OF ALL, thank you to the man behind Stalking Horse Press, James Reich. He is a brilliant editor and publisher, one of the most important writers in this country, and my friend. I am excited to be a part of the Stalking Horse family with Hannah Levbarg, Duncan Barlow, Jennifer McBain-Stephens, D. Foy, Jason De Boer, Kurt Baumeister, and Quintan Ana Wikswo.

ABOUT JORDAN A. ROTHACKER

Jordan A. Rothacker is the author of three novels: *The Pit, and No Other Stories* (2015), *And Wind Will Wash Away* (2016), and *My Shadow Book* by Maawaam (2017). Rothacker attended Manhattanville College in Purchase, NY before going on to receive a Masters in Religion and a PhD in Comparative Literature at the University of Georgia. His essays, fiction, poetry, book reviews, and interviews have appeared in such publications as *The Exquisite Corpse, Stone Highway Review, The Believer, Heavy Feather Review, Dark Matter, Dead Flowers, Boned, Guernica Magazine, Literary Hub, May Day, As It Ought to Be,* and *Cleaver Mag.* He lives in Athens, Georgia with his family, dogs, and a cat named Whiskey (not the cat in the author photo for this book—Rothacker doesn't know that cat at all—but Whiskey isn't offended as she prefers anonymity).

CPSIA information can be obtained
at www.ICGtesting.com
Printed in the USA
FFHW022045051218
49769286-54249FF

9 780999 115268